William Earee

Lyrics of a Life

William Earee

Lyrics of a Life

ISBN/EAN: 9783744787321

Printed in Europe, USA, Canada, Australia, Japan

Cover: Foto ©Andreas Hilbeck / pixelio.de

More available books at **www.hansebooks.com**

IN ALL LOVE

ℑ Dedicate

THIS THE WORK OF MY LIFE

TO

MY DEAR CHILDREN

AND TO THE MEMORY OF

MY EVER LOVED AND MOST

FONDLY CHERISHED

WIFE.

Rev. WILLIAM EARÉE.

(On his 80th birthday.)

Lyrics of a Life

By the

Rev. William Earée

Rector of Alphamstone, Essex.

EDINBURGH

PRINTED BY

BANKS & CO.

1896.

Preface.

• • •

IN the following Poems there is no bond of connection one with another—no continuous story or thread of narrative running through them all. Their composition extends over a period of between sixty and seventy years. A few of them were written in the early teens of the Author, others in maturer life, and some, "*The Songs of Nature,*" were written, most of them in his eightieth and eighty-second years.

This will account for the juvenile simplicity of some of the Poems, and the somewhat deeper strain and more reflective character of others.

However, whatever their respective merits or demerits, they are now sent forth to the Public just as they are, and not without the hope that, as the subjects are so various and their styles so different, there may be something to suit the various classes of readers, and so interest the younger and older generations alike.

Introductory Stanzas on some of the Contents.

• • •

Through these numbers run two ages—
  Mine in boyhood, mine in years;
Both I've written for these pages,
  Some with gladness, some with tears.

Here, by gorgeous hallow'd shrine,
  Falls Hypatia—martyr'd maid;
Pyramus and Thisbe pine,
  And Goliath low is laid.

Here a River winds, careering
  On through jungles, cities, plains;
Eagles round their eyries veering,
  Serpents glisten, lion reigns.

Here "The Prince's" welcome's given;
  Mighty Forests spread their shade;
Here's a Lunatic's grand Heaven,
  Where her pets with Angels play'd.

On the mount a Pilgrim falls—
  All the Winter he lies there;
Scarlet Lady here appals—
  Greatest Powers her curses scare.

Flickers here the midnight flash—
  Echo boomings of the Sea;
And the "Storm's" resounding crash—
  Grand, how grand, its revelry!

Here are "Angel, Child, and Flower,"
Ancient Cities 'neath their tombs;
Lovely girls' poetic bower—
Maidens flushed with freshest blooms.

In these lines triumphal tread
Conqueror-troops returning home,
Leaving thousand comrades dead,
Where the Ghosts of Grief will roam.

Here a "Nun and Lover" flirt—
Here "Star-gazers" search the Fates;
"Visions" scare, but do not hurt;
"Demos" opes the "Electorate" gates.

Lies in some a hapless Ship
Stranded on a rock-bound shore;
And a Skeleton in Time's grip
Full three thousand years or more.

Here the "Songs of Nature" rise—
Morning, Eventide, and Night;
Earth and Sea and starry Skies,
Lit with constellations bright.

Here are Stanzas-Juvenilia—
Efforts of my rhyming teens,
Mingling . . . well . . . with some Senilia,
And the Muse's statelier queens.

Reader now, and Critic, too—
Arbiters of rhymers' lot—
On these lines I pass to you,
To be remembered or forgot.

Contents.

• • •

PAGE

Introductory Stanzas .   ix

PART I.

NATIONAL REJOICINGS.

The Queen's Jubilee 3

Return of the Prince of Wales from India:
Welcome Home—a National Greeting . . 5

Triumphal Entry of the German Armies into
Berlin at the close of the Franco-German
War 9

PART II.

The Great India Contractor   15

PART III.

SONGS OF NATURE.

Song of the Morning . .   27

Song of the Evening . .   30

Song of the Night . .   33

PAGE

Song of the Earth . . . 37
Song of the Sky 41
Song of the Clouds . . . 46
Song of the River 49
Song of the Sea 53
Song of the Wind 56
Song of the Forest 60
Song of the Spirit of Beauty . . . 66
Song of the Church 68
Song of the Flowers 71
Love's Own Song. 75
Song of Death 77
Hunger Personified 80

PART IV.

A TALE IN VERSE.

The Hop-picker . . 85

PART V.

MISCELLANEOUS POEMS.

A Throng of Mountains : Their Glorious
    Grandeur 117
The "Astræa" 124
Meleager's Lament at the Tomb of Heleodora . 127
Farewell 129
On the Death of Prince Henry of Battenberg . 130

Contents.

xiii

	PAGE
Australia	133
Old London	135
Old England (Song of Her Patriots)	139
Stanzas, partly in Northern Dialect	141
The Mountain Pilgrim of Cumberland	144
On a Skeleton (dug up near Scarboro' in 1834)	146
"Did the contempt of families terrify me?" (Job xxxi. 34)	148
Rudolph Parting from Hilda	150
The Buried Miners	152
Still They Sleep	154
The Octogenarian	156
The Scarlet Lady: A Vision	157
The Contrast: A Dialogue	160
The Windmill	162
The Dear Old Fire	164
He thinks He hears their Echoes	166
She fell like a Flower	168
Angel, Child, and Flower: A Trilogue—Xmas	171
The Flower-Girl	173
The Stranded Ship (Fact)	175
The Life-Boat Crew	177
Yesterday	179
The Poor Old Horse	181
The War-Horse—France: An Allegory	184
Plaint of the Convicts' Child	186
The Midnight Storm	188

	PAGE
Johnnie and Jeannie, Workhouse Children: A Christmas Dialogue	190
A Father's Farewell	193
The Old Oak	196
Demos; or, The New Electorate	197
The Present Distress	200
The Anarchists	203
Hester, the Lunatic	206
The Despondent Maiden	208
Willie and Maggie (Horace, Book III., Ode 9—Free Translation)	212
Lay of the Engine-Driver	214
The Finger-Post	219
The Village	220
The Contrast	222
The Watchers of the Deep (Founded on Fact)	224
Water or Wine?	226
The Fireman	227
The Nun and her Lover	229
The Mechanics of England	230
Plaint of the Widowed Queen (Adelaide)	232
Herod's Funeral	233
Elegy	234
Lauretta (From the Italian)	237
Julia B.: A Great Beauty	238
Old Norwich: A Fragment	239
The Ride to a Wedding	241
Any Pans, Sir?	244

PAGE

The Old Newspaper 246
An Old Man stood in an Old Churchyard . 247
The Sculptor's Vision 248
Hibernia (Rival Candidates for her Love) . 249
Love on a Lake 251
Cradle for the First-born 252
Then They must Go 255

PART VI.

CITIES OF THE PAST.

Ancient Athens 259
Jerusalem: A Fragment . . . 265
Babylon: A Fragment . . . 268

PART VII.

LIBRETTI FOR CANTATAS.

Pyramus and Thisbe 273
David and Goliath 301
Hypatia 320

PART I.

• • •

National Rejoicings.

A

The Queen's Jubilee.

● ● ●

WITH gladness thrills all England's heart,
  Earth's greatest Queen, for thee,
And, jubilant, the land will keep
  Thy golden Jubilee!
Ye millions, loyal to her sway,
  High let your voices rise!
Let all the nation's plaudits swell
  Loud echoing to the skies!

" The mother of our kings to be,"
  Round whom our love has grown,
As woman, parent, ruler, Queen,
  She honours England's throne.
Her heart goes forth to lowliest roofs,
  No less than grandeur's domes;
Her messages of love she speeds
  To hearths of humblest homes.

The Colonies—a glorious group,
  Outspread o'er every sea—
Her distant children hail with us
  Victoria's Jubilee;

While princes, powers, and potentates
  And patriots of nations,
The gallant chivalry of each
  Send gifts and gratulations.

Then let our hills all peal aloud
  From every tower and steeple—
Our armaments all boom to hail
  The mother of her people!
Let banners wave and pennons fly,
  And drums and trumpets sound;
Let all our voices grandly roll
  In cheers the nation round!

Before our altars, bright and loved,
  Be priest and people seen,
To bless the God who fifty years
  Has blessed our gracious Queen.
And for "*Memorial*" be our aim
  To cheer the poor for ages—
A tribute higher than poet's song,
  Than eulogy of sages.

May long her light illume the throne—
  Her evening light so pure!
Her glorious reign in scrolls of fame,
  Bright historied, shall endure.
Then England, let thy millions shout:
  "Hail, Queen of a people free!"
We keep this day, all jubilant,
  Thy glorious Jubilee!

• • •

Welcome Home.

(A NATIONAL GREETING.)

• • •

HOME, home he comes!—From India's shore
  Resounds "God speed him well!"
A thousand, thousand voices cheer—
  "Good-bye, good Prince,—farewell!"
Waft, waft him then, O England!
  Across the water's foam,
From hearts and hearths all jubilant,
  The welcome of his home.

Chorus—

> He comes, he comes, God bless him!
>   Lov'd round the rolling earth;
> Ring all thy bells to greet him,
>   Land of his love and birth!

He comes with India's many Powers
 Bound round the Imperial throne
With closer ties than battling hosts
 Could e'er have bound alone.
Yes, pilgrim Prince, thy manly grace
 Was magical—its spell
More triumphs won o'er India's realms
 Than e'er could shot or shell !

Chorus—

> Then let us sing, " God bless him ! "
> Lov'd round the rolling earth ;
> Rise, Britain, rise to hail him,
> Land of his pride and birth !

Before him Chiefs and Potentates,
 A gemm'd and brilliant crowd,
With gorgeous blazonries and state
 In humble homage bow'd ;
And mighty Peoples, many-tongued,
 Press'd on his march of Fame—
Idolaters of many Gods
 Prais'd high his royal Name.

Chorus—

> Then let us sing, " God bless him ! "
> Lov'd round the rolling earth ;
> Rise, Britain, rise to hail him,
> Land of his pride and birth !

Marvell'd the millions One so great,
  Star of Imperial courts,
The honoured one of England's love
  Should join their native sports !
Boldly he sought the lion's haunt,
  Boldly the tiger's lair,
The serpent's path, the jungle's depths,
  The elephant hid there !

Chorus—

> Then let us sing, "God bless him !"
>   Lov'd round the rolling earth ;
> Rise, Britain, rise to hail him,
>   Land of his pride and birth !

He saw where Mutiny had kept
  Its holiday of blood—
In carnival of slaughter, slew
  The beautiful and good !
He saw the pomp of altars proud
  And cult of many a shrine,
And longed for messengers of peace
  To shew the way Divine.

Chorus—

> Then let us sing, "God bless him !
>   Lov'd round the rolling earth ;
> Rise, Britain, rise to hail him,
>   Land of his pride and birth !

"Beats high" (he said) "my England's heart,
  O India, warm for thee !
The bearer of her great good-will
  I'm proud and bless'd to be."
And "nobly is his mission done,"
  Say, some recording dome !
Now, back he comes for needed rest
  At home—at home—sweet home !

Chorus—

Then let us sing, "God bless him ! "
  Lov'd round the rolling earth ;
Rise, Britain, rise to hail him,
  Land of his pride and birth !

O England, then, to greet him back,
  High welcome let him see !
The throne, and wife, and all at home,
  How deep *their* joy will be !
Ye patriots glad all round the land
  Lift up the loud acclaim,
And thunder forth his laurel-crown'd,
  His far-resounding fame !

Chorus—

Then let us sing, "God bless him !
  Lov'd round the rolling earth ;
Ring all thy bells to hail him,
  Land of his love and birth !

Triumphal Entry of the German Armies into Berlin at the close of the Franco-German War.

∙ ∙ ∙

DAY of triumph! Palms and bays
Crown Berlin this day of days!
Home her warrior-legions march
Underneath her Linden-Arch.
Pennons flutter, standards wave,
Flags and banners greet her brave;
Chargers, proud and prancing, neigh—
Flaunt the head with ribbons gay,
Spread their nostrils, paw the air,
Marching home in conquest's glare—
Sword and helmet, spear and lance,
Bear the brunt of humbled France!

"Welcome home!" the cannons roar,
Now the giant strife is o'er;
Bells from towers a "welcome" sound,
"Welcome!" cry all things around.
Voice of bugles, beat of drum,
Voice—*no* voice this day is dumb.

Blast of trumpets, piercing thrill,
Clang of clarions spread the thrill.
Welcome home, ye legions grand—
Welcome home to Father Land !
German love with honour now
Yearns to deck each warrior's brow.

Seas of voices grandly roll
Waves of welcome—billowed soul !
Battlements with shoutings high
Hail the conquerors passing by !
Balconies, where throng the fair,
Sweet jubilations echo there.
Marching on the cohorts go,
Scanned above and scanned below ;
Eyes intently yearn to greet
" One " they never more will meet—
" One " that slumbers far away
In that Night that knows no Day.

Yet as on and on they tread
Many find their lov'd . . . *not* dead !
Greetings ring at every turn,
Hearts to hearts responsive burn.
" Welcome, father ! "—" welcome, brother ! "—
" Welcome, son ! " acclaims the mother.
Echoing far in thunder loud,
" Moltke ! Moltke ! " shouts the crowd—

" Bismarck !" heir of deathless fame,
Loud they swell that mighty name—
Louder still, if that could be
" His," their prince of chivalry,
Finest of the hero band,
Eldest son of Father Land !
" Welcome, Unser Fritz !" they cry—
" Welcome !" echoes back the sky.

PART II.

• • •

The Great India Contractor.

THOMAS CRAIGIE GLOVER, Esq.

The Great India Contractor.

• • •

THOMAS CRAIGIE GLOVER, Esq.

(*The Brassey of the East.*)

• • •

GREAT the magic of his Name
  In India's Archives traced,
Chronicled by grateful hands
  Where *'twill not* be effaced;
Styled the Brassey of the East
  (That Star of Engineers),
Both renowned in many lands,
  Both great in equal spheres.

Mightiest marvels hath he wrought
  In India's glowing land,
Where, through rocks, ravines and hills,
  Her Railway routes were planned.
Kindled there, his lamp of fame
  All through the East doth glow,
Thousand thousands, East and West,
  His Railway wonders know,

Rivers rushing wild and deep,
 Unbridged, he bridged with strength,
Many and wide their graceful spans
 And picturesque their length.
Vain the force of headlong floods !—
 To shake them . . . floods are vain ;
Like the rocks, unmoved they stand !
 Like rocks, they will remain !

Great and famed the Glorious Dock
 That bears the Prince's [1] name !
Weak the wrestling power of Seas
 To break its solid frame !
Mighty though the Ocean-storms,
 And mighty though the gale,
Harbouring *here* all ships are safe,
 For *here* no storms assail !

Here, what varied flags will fly
 O'er cargoes from all climes !—
Here, what freights will Nations send
 Far down to distant times !

---

[1] Prince's Dock, Bombay, the area of which is 30 acres, was so called because the Prince of Wales laid the foundation-stone, 11th November 1875. It was opened by the Governor of Bombay, 1st January 1880.

Ships with tattered sails and shrouds
  To this Great Dock will go,
And some, with flaunting streamers gay,
  Sublime in bulk and show.

Works of mortal men are brief
  But some immortal stay,
This is one—built strong to last—
  Refusing to decay.
Great in me my pride would be
  If *I* such work could frame,
Which to ages far remote
  Will hand down Glover's name.

Theme for wonder, long to come,
  The Reservoir[1] will be—
Vast and grand! a Glorious Work!
  An "Aqua Pura" Sea!
Marvellous its giant wall,
  Its width and depth profound!
Wonderful its lofty height,
  And steadfast as the ground!

---

[1] The Tansa Dam enclosing the Reservoir is 2 miles long, 115 feet
high, and 103 feet thick at the bottom, and the area of the Reservoir
is 8 square miles in extent.   It is 60 miles from Bombay.   The water
is carried the whole of that 60 miles in pipes.

It is one of the most stupendous pieces of engineering the world
has ever known.

Crystal seems this glassy Lake,
  Oft grand with golden light;
Impotent the waves against
  Its Masonry of might.
Hence, though centuries come and go,
  Though thousand years pass by,
Firm this Reservoir will last
  And age on age defy!

As Contractor, far is told
  The story of his deeds—
Grand, magnificent, sublime,
  Supplying India's needs.
Merchandise of Nations great,
  Where *late* 'twas never seen,
Now is brought for millions there,
  All subjects of our Queen.

Men by myriads[1] he trained
  In railway work to toil,
Using mattock, axe and spade
  Like those who till the soil.

---

[1] More than 500,000 men have passed through his hands and become, many of them, through his effectual supervision and management, skilful workmen though *altogether unskilled before.* As, in addition to his many other great works, he constructed more than 1200 miles of railway, these immense multitudes were indispensable, and needed special skill to discipline and instruct them in their work.

Gold he won, devoting much
    To bless his workmen's lot—
Glorying most in doing good
    Which cannot be forgot.

Like the King in days of old,
    With sceptre in his hand,
Visiting the Harvest-Field
    To incite the reaping band—
So did *He*, as Railway-King,
    Among his workmen go,
Train and pay, befriend and guide,
    And kindly help bestow.

Famine [1] once appalled the land,
    With direful sway it raged;
Great the crowds of famished men,
    Their hunger unassuaged.
Scores of thousands he employed
    And thousands daily fed;
His the hand that succoured all,
    Or numbers had been dead!

---

[1] Scindia Railway—Great Viaduct over the River Chambul. While Mr Glover was constructing this, many thousands of famine-stricken people came to the work to be fed, and were entirely supported by Mr Glover at his own expense for a considerable time.

Glad the eye that saw his face,
  The ear that heard his voice,—
All that saw and heard him near
  Would thank him and rejoice.
For all the famine-stricken hosts
  That cried in their distress,
Opened was his bounteous hand,
  And pitying heart to bless.

Thus "*Railway Systems*," reaching far,
  And linking Lines remote;
Viaducts o'er valleys deep,
  The *Dock* with ships afloat;
Rivers spanned on every hand—
  What stately Bridges there!
Such are some of many Works
  He wrought with Genius rare.

India is his 'scutcheon grand,
  His Heraldry is there:
Blazoned brightly on that Shield
  His "Arms" She'll ever wear—
Not in transient "Quarterings" gilt,
  Or mouldering marble graved,
But in glorious Works enshrined
  For which e'en Death[1] he braved.

---

[1] In the earlier stages of his career, when India was far less civilised than it is now, three fanatical attempts were made on his life.

Deeds like his and works so vast
  Will keep his Memory green,
Written on the Scroll of Fame,
  'Mid names illustrious seen;
Though decay o'er Nations sweep,
  As on the ages run,
India yet will ever *share*
  The triumphs he has won.

𝕬ppendix to 𝕻oem.

LIST OF A FEW OF THE WORKS EXECUTED BY MR GLOVER.

---

1. Foreshore Reclamation, Bombay.   Area reclaimed 200 acres.

2. Carnac, Musjid and Elphinstone Over-Bridges, Bombay. These bridges span 4 lines of rail.   Difficult foundations.

3. Doubling portion G.I.P. Railway between Egutpora and Bhosawul Railway—70 miles, Broad Gauge.

4. Mhow - ke - Mulla Viaduct, Bhore Ghat, G.I.P. Railway. Re-opening communication over the immense ravine into which it had fallen.   Receiving telegraphic notice of fall in middle of night when in bed ; by 9.30 A.M. he was on his way to repair it with 2000 men and all requisites— tents, tools, provisions, &c.   Finished the great work in 10 days.

5. Reconstruction of the Mhow-ke-Mulla Viaduct, Bhore Ghat, G.I.P. Railway.

6. Portion of B.B. and C.I. Railway (Broad Gauge) between Veerangaum and Wudwan.

7. Taptee Viaduct, carrying G.I.P. Railway over Taptee River, constructed entirely of iron.   Has 32 spans.

8. Government Railway between Agra and Ajmere and Nusser-abad—286 miles in length. Large Viaduct across River Jumna; foundations **70** feet *below bed* of the *River.*

9. Prince's Dock, Bombay.—*See* Poem. Foundation-stone laid by H.R.H. the Prince of Wales, being the first public ceremony performed by him in India.

10. Scindia State Railway (for Government), Broad Gauge. Large Viaduct across the River Chambul; foundations in wells 80 feet below river bed. Many thousands of famine-stricken people came to this work to be fed, and were entirely supported for a considerable time by Mr Glover.—*See* Poem.

11. Bhopal State Railway (for Government), Broad Gauge. Large Bridge across Nerbudda River; entailed almost continuous rock-cuttings 50 to 60 feet deep.

12. Railway from Gwalior to Thansi (Broad Gauge), including large Bridge across the Sindh River and some very heavy rock-cuttings.

13. Railway from Etawah to Sangor. Portion of I.M. Railway, including a very large rock-cutting.

14. Tansa Dam (of masonry). This Masonry Dam is the largest in existence.—*See* Poem.

MINOR WORKS FOR THE MUNICIPALITY OF BOMBAY.

1. Bombay Markets at Boru Bunder.
2. Bombay Abattoirs at Bundora.

3. Large Drain across Flats, including Pumping Station at Worlee.

4. Null Bazaar (Market).

5. Vehar Lake (Bombay Water Supply). Saved Bombay from what might have been a water famine.

6. The Crawford Markets, Bombay.

And many other Works for the G.I.P. Railway.

PART III.

• • •

Songs of Nature.

Song of the Morning.

• • •

I ROBE myself in glory,
  I splash the East with gold,
Unfurl my scarlet banners,
  Put out each twinkling world;
          With gorgeous hues
          Besprent with dews,
I robe myself in glory.

I make all things look fresher,
  The green grass still more green,
The brightest things still brighter,
  And lovelier every scene;
          The mists of night
          Dissolve in flight,
As I robe myself in glory.

As up I rise all smiling,
  What music fills the air?
The songs of God's musicians,
  All singing everywhere!
          Their hymns of praise
          To God they raise,
As I robe myself in glory.

With dews my garments shimmer,
 All fresh with breath of flowers,
As I walk among the gardens,
 Perfuming all their bowers;
   The earth, the air,
   Look always gayer,
As I robe myself in glory.

"Would God that it were Morning!"
 How many sick ones say!
And when I come, they hail me
 The longed-for "Peep-of-Day;"
   What welcome sight
   To them my light,
As I robe myself in glory.

As o'er the dim horizon
 I lift my blushing face,
The wildest beasts go slinking,
 Each to his hiding-place;
   All then give o'er
   Their growl or roar,
When I robe myself in glory.

Earth's sleepers hear me calling
 From out the rosy skies,
Shake off their nightly slumbers,
 And greet me as they rise;
   They start each day
   With work or play,
As I robe myself in glory.

If I wake with eyelids weeping,
  My tears impearl the ground;
Snow-wreaths in winter weaving,
  I wreathe on all things round;
        More sparkling glows
        This work of snows,
When I robe myself in glory.

The mighty hills eternal,
  I earliest flood with light,
And crown their brows with coronals
  Just flickering into sight;
        I tip their spires
        With Orient fires,
When I robe myself in glory.

I beautify the mountains,
  The earth, the sea, the air,
The grand and glorious temple,
  The village house of prayer;
        All look their best,
        As if new-blest,
When I robe myself in glory.

Thus on and on for ages,
  Shall I each day begin,
Till earth's last morn has vanished,
  And ends the reign of sin;
        Then up the skies
        All saints shall rise,
To be robed by God in glory,
To be robed by God in glory.

Song of the Evening.

• • •

'MID hues of gorgeous splendour,
  I hover o'er the world,
And, spun by heavenly fingers,
  My cloud-robes hang unfurled;
      All down the sky
      My colours fly,
Adorning earth and heaven.

I bring a halcyon stillness;
  I hush all nature round,
The fragrant gentle breezes,
  The voices of the ground;
      Soft purls the rill,
      While o'er the hill
The clouds in pomp are moving.

The birds of thousand woodlands,
  Sing me their evening song,
Then—One takes up the warbling,
  She sings the whole night long;
      She trills—She thrills,
      She thrills—She trills,
And fills the air with music,

And when I bring the rainbow—
  My coronet of heaven,
What pageantry of beauty
  To all the sky is given;
        Soft-dripping showers
        Impearl the flowers,
The groves, the grass, the gardens.

On rocks of olden ages
  My softening smile is bright,
The monarch-hills majestic
  I bathe in golden light;
        Thus I diffuse
        My richest hues,
And drape all things in glory.

The bells of village churches,
  How beautiful they sound,
I waft their blessèd voices
  O'er all the fields around;
        They swell—they die,
        They cease—they fly
Away to mystic dreamland.

No time so sweet as evening
  To youth and tender maid,
As through the lanes they wander,
  With hopes that soon may fade,
        Like scenes now bright
        With evening light,
But darkening ere the morning.

The children—romping, laughing,
  Released from toil or books—
I gladden in my radiance,
  I brighten all their looks;
      They dance, they sing
      Around their ring,
A joy to all who see them.

I enter solemn churchyards,
  With mourners lingering round,
I shine on all the tombstones,
  On every grassy mound;
      Some, by their dead
      Prefer to tread,
While I am smiling o'er them.

But when th' old sun is fading,
  I too shall quit the earth,
Nor longer cast my shadows
  On scenes of grief or mirth;
      And *then* shall rise
      'Neath brighter skies,
The day that knows no evening.

Song of the Night.

● ● ●

Hush—hush—I come, let Nature sleep,
As o'er the Heavens with gloom I sweep
    And Earth enfold ;
Yet list—for voices still are there
On sea and earth and in the air,
    Their words untold.

On every bough I hush the songs,
The nightly hymns of feathered throngs—
    Then, silence reigns.
On every bed would I could still
Each wail of sorrow and the thrill
    Of mortal pains.

Oft while my darkling hours pass by,
Weird, shadowy visions some descry
    Of ghostly mien,
With noiseless footsteps pacing o'er
Some moss-grown Abbey's Corridor,
    And dread the scene.

c

I drape not always Earth in gloom,
But brighten many a shrine and tomb
    And temple-nave :
On mourners, soft the beams I shed,
As, sad, they bend the low-bowed head
    O'er humble grave.

And when I shimmer down my light
Of moon or starry heavens bright,
    Then lovers stroll,
And thank me for the blissful scene,
Whose spell of tenderest softened sheen
    Enchants their soul.

When Heaven and Earth from sight I shroud,
When not a star peers through a cloud,
    Let toilers rest ;
My hours are theirs—let them be free,
'Tis mine to give them liberty,
    'Tis God's behest.

Though oft I *hide*, I oft *reveal*
What daylight's glowing clouds conceal—
    The stellar world.
Come, mortal doubter, ope' thine eyes
As I unveil the starry skies,—
    Look up—behold !

System on system—star on star—
Whose myriads roll through space afar;
　　Say, doubter, say—
Who gave these lamps eternal light
And speeds their everlasting flight,
　　Poor child of clay?

'Tis when my murkiest shadows fall,
Men muffle with my sable pall
　　Their darkest deeds:
My clouded vault oft echoes then,
When, smitten by remorseless men,
　　Some victim bleeds.

In Midnight thunders as I go,
With flashing lightning-flames I glow
　　And scare the world.
In storm-clouds sing my midnight-choir,
As wild I play with bolts of fire
　　From heaven hurled.

Of wandering ships I thwart the way
With billowed mountains, wild with play
　　Of towering crest:
Or, looking down with silvery light,
With breathless calm I still the night
　　And lull its rest.

c 3

Soft wordless voices all around
Chant through my Night-Hall's mighty bound,
    Unheard their tone;
Yet *other* voices, loud and long,
I weave into my midnight song,
    To God alone.

I stop the rage of battle-roar,—
Then, Death's dread Carnival is o'er,
    While, dark, I reign:
Yet still what prostrate heroes moan;
On blood-stained grass how loud the groan
    Of harrowing pain!

With stars withdrawn—no moon—no light,
I come—I come—great ebon Night
    My watch to keep:
With my all-spreading, outstretched wings
God shadows out the sight of things
    For Nature's sleep.

Sad, dying beds I curtain round,
And hush to silence every sound,
    While Life is closing:
A brooding spell of awe I shed
In solemn chambers of the dead
    So still reposing.

Song of the Earth.

• • •

LAUNCHED swiftly through th' Eternal sky
As on I rush, and float, and fly,
   God's wondrous works I bear:
All islands, forests, rivers, plains,
My mountains vast, my billowy mains,
   My all-surrounding air.

On, on for many thousand years
Beneath yon mystic, starry spheres,
   Along my path I've rolled:
And *shall* for countless thousands more
Through depths of space that know no shore
   And systems vast enfold.

Though nestling in my *bosom*, sleep
Dread brooding forces, yet to leap
   In thunder, flame, and might;
Still on my *face* I weave the smiles
Of blushing blooms and playful wiles,
   Of sweetly laughing light.

The canticles of feathered throngs,
The holy praise of children's songs
 Up from my orb ascend,
And *with* them, oft the bridal bell
And solemn toll of funeral knell,
 Along my pathway blend.

The bones and dust of Nations lost,
To dark oblivion, doomed and tossed,
 I carry through the sky ;
And *with* them, all the crowds that sleep
In churchyard-chambers, still and deep,
 Long mourned with many a sigh.

By man oft citied, towered and domed,
What *now* such works? Some as I've roamed
 Like transient bubbles blown !
What crumbling of his domes and towers,
His palaced cities—how like flowers—
 Long perished and unknown !

Yes ! 'neath my dust old cities lie,
And none may e'er the site descry
 Where once their glory shone :
And e'en the *Nations*, proud and great,
That raised them in their sculptured state,
 They too as dreams are gone.

Convulsions great in epochs past—
I bear their vestiges, to last
   Till heaven and earth shall flee.
In rock and mountain, sea and ground,
The venerable wrecks abound
   Of things no more to be.

As down hath rolled Time's ceaseless flood,
O'er red Aceldamas of blood,
   I've spread my verdant pall;
No marble tells one hero's name,
No page records his death or fame—
   My turf now covers all.

Mid all the planets of the sky,
Was e'er one honoured such as I—
   The choice of Christ—the God,
For down from heaven He came to me,
And on my deserts, plains, and sea,
   His holy feet once trod.

As once He hung on Calvary's height,
With darkness wrapt as 'twere of night,
   I bore Him, tortured, slain;—
At such a sight my mountains shake,
And my great solid globe did quake.
   What . . . when He comes again?

All olden curses then subdued,
With radiance I shall be *renewed*,
    With beauty mantled round ;
No frown of God from yonder sky,
No falling tear from human eye,
    O'er vanished ones—no mound.

All round my orb may angels then
Walk mingling with the sons of men,
    Heaven's Holy Ones with *mine ;*
Whilst I no more shall bear a tomb,
But flourish with immortal bloom,
    Made glorious and divine !

New Heavens, too, will yield their light,
Forever beautiful, and bright
    With scenes none yet can know ;—
Then *I*, the *Earth*, the *Heavens*, and *Man*,
Shall *all* be changed in God's new plan,
    And all with splendour glow !

Let hallelujahs bright to Heaven
By all night-voices joined be given,
    For they in truth are mine ;
I soften, mingle, tune them all
In praise to Him who made them all,—
    The gracious Power divine.

Song of the Sky.

• • •

THE Pavilion of Nature high,
  I spread my mighty dome
O'er the worlds of my thousand heavens
  That *there* forever roam:
In my concave the planets play
  Through orbits vast and bright,
And the comets career forever
  Through voids of depth and height.

In my coronet gleam the stars;—
  I weave my vapoury fold
Now in ripples of silvery sheen
  And now in amber and gold;
In my circuits the lightning revels,
  Great thunders roll their peals,
But their revelries soon are spent
  In my boundless, starry fields.

Not the angels with rushing wings,
  Whom God afar may send
In their travels of ceaseless speed
  Can find in me an *end.*

Nor can that which is swifter still
  (For what so swift as light),
Any bound ever reach in me
  Eternal though its flight !

Yet my vastness is *full of God*,[1]
  The ever-present Lord,
Who but speaks, and His thousand hosts
  Fly min'st'ring all abroad ;
Though my firmaments stretch forever,
  Through *all*, pervading *there*,
In His Spirit of living power
  He is ever everywhere.

Constellations as flags I hang
  Deep streaming down my sky,
And my banners of shining worlds
  I float and wave on high :
I emblazon my 'scutcheons there
  With heraldry of God,
And I marshal ethereal fires
  Where angels never trod.

Oh, ye Suns, in your glories blaze,
  Blaze on through countless years,
Ye, to *Me*, are but *specks* in size,
  Mere *sparks* your blazing spheres.

---

[1] Omnia sunt plena Jovis.—*Virgil.*

Oh, ye Stars, I have heights and depths
  Where broods eternal night,
Though ye swarm in your myriads far,
  And spread your streams of light.

High in massed and radiant clouds
  My airy towers I shape,
And the walls of my castles there
  With golden ivy drape;
I have bowers recessed in air,
  And burnished thrones of pearl
Where aerial beings sit
  And their cloudy trains unfurl.

With my shadowy armies ranged
  In gleaming, wild array,
With Auroras from measureless heights
  That flicker o'er the fray,
With the spectres I shape in clouds
  (My phantom fiends of air);
With these ominous, weird portents
  Earth's gazers oft I scare.

Not the length of all æons could tell
  How vast—how grand my age;
For with me is no time—and none
  My depth of years could gauge.

Not the roll of the times of God
  Can ever exceed my own,
For with both, 'tis "Eternal Now,"
  Though million years have flown.

Yes, Eternity yet to come
  Will find me fresh as now,
For no ages can ever write
  Their wrinkles on my brow :
From my vault they can never pluck
  One sphere through heaven hurled,
Or arrest in my empyrean
  The smallest flying world.

But the hour of Doom will come,
  For gathering all in me,
When the "Trumpet of God" shall shake
  My vast infinity :
When, careering through countless spheres,
  The Cherubim shall fly,
And the rushing of seraph-wings
  Resound through me, the Sky.

O'er the scene of assembled hosts
  Of all men ever born,
Shall I spread my boundless arch
  That Resurrection morn—

For the *Saints* must I open up
  The corridors of bliss,
For the *lost* must I deepen down
  A sorrowful abyss.

Then my Song of the Sky shall blend
  With songs the angels sing,
With the swell of their shouts that then
  Shall through Creation ring—
Then the choirs of the human race,
  Upsprung from 'neath the sod,
With my Song of the Sky shall blend
  All jubilant of God.

Song of the Clouds.

• • •

On our fleecy wings We started
  Round the earth through space to fly,
On the day when fresh created,
  Swift she rolled along the sky:
Thousand, thousand ages gone,
  Saw Our floating glory's flight,
With its streams of golden beauty,
  With its silvery wreaths of light.

All those slowly creeping ages
  We have swept o'er seas and ground,
Coroneted mountain monarchs,
  Highest hills with grandeur crowned.
Now, We've clothed the earth with snow;
  Now, with dews impearled the flowers,
Filled the rillets, brooks and rivers,
  Freshened air and earth with showers.

Swaddling-bands of the Great Thunder,
  Oft We wage terrific powers,
Cradling too the awful Lightning,
  Crashing crags and forts and towers,

We with flames and deluge bursting,
  Flood the vales—the forest fire;
Let the whirlwind loose for havoc,
  Roll the echoes of Our choir.

As We glide 'neath songs of heaven,
  Floating o'er the songs of earth,
Bless'd the strains of saints *above* Us,—
  Wails *below* oft mock its mirth.
Some have feigned that We are chariots
  Bearing angels through the air,
Brightening Us with their own splendour,
  Beautiful beyond compare.

Water-drops which We distil
  Richest vineyards turn to wine,
Wine full meet for cups of gold
  And the holy cup divine.
Showers We shed, transmuted thus,
  Princes quaff 'mid grandeurs great,
These in gorgeous banquets glow,
  Rich in blazonry of state.

High ascending, oft We soar
  Up and up the boundless skies—
Fainter grows Our softening radiance,
  Thinner, fainter, as We rise;—
Up We soar till, scarcely seen,
  High and higher upwards driven,
Mounting like the souls of saints,
  Till We vanish into heaven,

Shadowy armies oft We show
 Fiercely raging in the sky,
Grand their hosts of dazzling flame,
 Flaunting blazing standards high :
Downward stream the crimson torrents
 Upward smokes the battle-pyre ;
Vast the warriors, bright and mighty,
 Burning with intensest fire.

See! in Us, God sets His Bow,
 Signet of His Truth divine,
Arch of *Witness*—arch of beauty,
 Ages past have known its Sign ;
Ages hence shall see its circlet
 Set in Us by God's own hand,
Telling out, His Word is sure
 In every age—to every land.

Unimagined glory waits Us—
 "Lo, He comes with *clouds !*" 'tis said ;
Thousand thousands wait before Him—
 All the living—all the dead.
We, His *clouds*, shall then attend Him
 Floating round the judgment scene,
More illumined then with glory
 Than We ever yet have been.

Song of the River.

• • •

I was born on the mountains
  Of the springs and the dew,
Where the lightnings are volleyed,
  And the great thunders brew.
Softly dripping in shadow,
  Gaily trickling in sight,
I descend their proud summits
  Like a thin thread of light.

Thus in dripping and trickling
  To a rillet I grow,
And then, rippling in music,
  On my journey I go.
In my progress while sweeping
  Through meadows and plains,
Do I gather the brooklets,
  And I gather the rains.

To the song of my gliding
  Through the glades and the dells,
They all give me their waters,
  And my tiny stream swells,

D

Till at last I'm a River
  And through continents flow,
Now in wild rushing rapids,
  Now majestic and slow.

Through the densest of forests
  Do I hold on my way;
Through the vastest of prairies
  With the bison I stray:
I go wandering through jungles
  'Midst the savages' homes,
Through the thunder of lions
  And where the elephant roams.

To the mightiest of cities
  Stately navies I bear,
And the lights of their glory
  Down my water-depths flare.
I pass by old cathedrals
  Where famed martyrs have trod,
There I hear the grand anthem
  Rise in glory to God.

In the dark I pass chambers
  Gay with dance and with song,
Whence have echoed sweet voices
  From the bright brilliant throng;
And I roam by the graveyards
  Of the ages gone bye,
Where their thousands of sleepers
  In forgetfulness lie.

On my margin have sauntered
  The fond youth and the maid;
Files of Nuns have meandered,
  Holy devotees prayed:
Loveliest daughters of beauty,
  While serenely I flow,
Lave their limbs in my waters,
  Fair and pure as the snow.

On my stream ride the Caiques
  Lined with velvet and gold,
Where the noblesse of nations
  Their silk pennants unfold;
On my stream rides the commerce
  Of all ships of the world,
And projectiles of battle
  In dread war to be hurled.

I have watered earth's deserts,
  And I water her isles;
And her continents stretching
  Lonely thousands of miles:
By the cottage, the palace,
  And the wigwam of palms,
I go rolling my waters
  In the storm and in calms.

I have flowers on my margin,
  That oft stoop to behold
Their rich beauty reflected
  All in crimson and gold.

I have shady seclusions
  For my fish that are shy,
And sedges for creatures
  That creep or that fly.

I glass back to the swan
  The proud curves of its grace
And the circuit of heaven,
  Both its stars and its space.
And the child o'er my borders,
  Looking down in its glee,
Sees its *own* image answered
  In my waters by me.

Broad and deep ever growing,
  On and onward I go
Towards my home of the ocean,
  To which all rivers flow.
All my course have I wandered
  To spread blessings on man,
To the swell of my ending
  From the drop I began.

So let man on his journey
  To Eternity's shore,
To do good all around him
  Learn of me evermore:
Be the path of his mission
  More florescent with love,
Till it end in high heaven,
  The bright region above.

Song of the Sea.

• • •

A REALM of death—yet full of life,
  From age to age I roll;
Mysterious, vast, sublime, I march
  And sweep from pole to pole;—
With songs of ripples now I flow,
With roar of billows now I go,
By light of day—through nights of gloom,
Then back my tidal march resume,
  And thus I go forever.

God's voice is heard in all my waves—
  His power in all my deeps;
There, down in darkness, are the graves
  Where many a dear one sleeps:
There age and childhood long have laid,
The much-loved youth—the beauteous maid,
Where tear of mourner ne'er can reach,
Where bones unmemoried lie and bleach
  Unknown, unfound forever.

I mirror back the eternal stars
 That stud Creation's dome,
The sun that blazes 'neath the arch
 Where angels have their home,
The chariots in which the Almighty rides,
The burnished cloud through heaven that
  glides,
The lightning's flash—the thunder-pall—
For ages I've reflected all,
 And *shall* reflect forever.

Within my boundless depths are things
 Minute and vast and strange,
Their form bespeaks the "Mighty God"
 Who fills creation's range ;—
They play, devour, and swim and swarm
In shallows, billows—calm or storm—
Terrific, mild—in shoals—alone,
Or shrined far down in hidden stone—
 There fossilized forever.

And I have growths men wot not of
 In weed, and mud, and slime,
Growths that began in primal years,
 Coeval with all time;
And bards, with mythologic things,
Have filled my surges, depths, and springs
With water-gods and water-ghosts,
And sirens, haunting near my coasts,
 Fond myths that last forever.

But there is One whose power I own,
  The Christ of Galilee,
Who trod my waves and lulled my storms,
  Incarnate Deity !
Again He'll come when Time has fled,
And bid me yield back all my dead,
Though sleeping in my rocks and caves,
A thousand ages 'neath my waves,
  Like sleeping there forever.

Then up shall spring the priest, the king,
  With girlhood, manhood, age,
The lords " that were," the slave, the free,
  The untutored and the sage—
Then all shall rise beneath the skies
To go where no one ever dies,
And there shall be no more a Sea
When souls are wrecked eternally
  No more- no more forever !

Song of the Wind.

● ● ●

EVOLUTION !—Great sages,
  How was *I* first evolved?
Of my essence, the mystery
  Has your science yet solved?
Of my motions eccentric
  Have you found out the cause?
Of my going and coming
  Can you show forth the laws?

I am free in my wandering
  O'er the earth to sweep round;
On the land or the sea
  To my course there's no bound;
Not all nations combined
  To restrain me have might,
On and on unimpeded
  Still I go day and night.

All the clouds on my wings
  Do I bear in my train,
Whether casting their shadows
  Or dropping in rain;

Whether nursing the thunder
  By his red flashes riven,
Or in amber and gold,
  Adding beauty to heaven.

Here I waft a light feather
  Or a bubble or foam,
There I wrestle with columns
  That may pillar a dome;
With the softest of breezes
  I oft play amongst flowers,
Or with cyclones majestic
  Rend the mightiest of towers.

Is a city in flames,
  Then my fire-sheeted air
Fans and wraps its proud structures
  In their hot burning glare,
Till the towers and the domes
  And its palaces fall,
And the clouds all ablaze
  Are their red-glowing pall.

Then the sands of the desert
  Through long ages I blow,
Till great cities are buried
  Where no travellers know:
Thus old Babylon sank
  'Neath the eye of the world,
And now Nineveh lies
  'Neath the sands I have whirled.

Great the pomp of my fury
　When in tempests I fly,
And the sound of my rushing
　Shakes the earth and the sky;
Then the trees of the forests,
　Crashing down, strew the plain
Like a weird field of battle
　Thickly strewn with the slain.

In the belfry I moan,
　Loud through trumpets I speak,
In the flute softly warble,
　Through the fife shrilly shriek,—
From the organ, I swell
　Glorious anthems to God,
O'er the aisles where the dead
　Once adoringly trod.

The mane of the lion
　And the officer's plume,
The gold curls of a child
　And the wreath on a tomb—
While I lift them and sway them
　Now in gusts, now in calm,
I am murmuring the tones
　Of my mystical psalm.

In its beauty I spread
　The cloud-glory of morn,
And, like waves of the sea,
　Often billow the corn;

While the smoke of the cottage
  I curl up o'er the trees,
And the music of steeples
  Floats afar on my breeze.

Gently stirring the pines,
  Softly wafting the snow,
Or the blossoms of spring
  As serenely I blow,
So, with leaves of the autumn,
  Overspreading the ground,
Do I rustle the voice
  Of mortality round.

I go down into gardens,
  Through the sweet-scented grove;
Over beds of rich spices
  Slow meandering I rove;
There my wings I oft batne
  In the fragrance of flowers,
Which as dews I then sprinkle
  On love-haunted bowers.

Thus my mission I fill
  As the agent of God,
Whether wandering through cities
  Or where man never trod;
He has made me a power,
  The great world's vital breath,
The fresh life of all things,—
  Without me, all were death!

Song of the Forest.

• • •

In the depths of the twilight
  Of the ages gone past
Did I flourish majestic,
  And to ages may last;
Before man was created
  I long, long had my birth,
And am now in all regions
  Round the orbit of earth.

Erst the ancients adored me
  Where their gods had their homes,
And I shrouded their temples
  Unsurmounted by domes:
The dense depths and the silence
  Of my far-spreading gloom
Gave an awe to their worship,
  Deep and grave as the tomb.

In my caves did the Druids,
  In the epochs of old,
Teach the children of nobles
  (A quaint scene to behold);

In my caves have their augurs
  The dim future unfurled,
And their priests offered victims
  Shadowed dark from the world.

Once were monarchs my patrons,
  They prescribed me my bound;
For me hamlets and churches
  Were razed to the ground;
Then the buck and the boar
  Were proud royalty's game,
And the doom of the poacher
  Was the ordeal of flame.

I have coverts of darkness
  Which the sun cannot pierce,
Where, in glooms of their hiding,
  Lurk the things that are fierce;
Lordly lions are my children,
  As the breeze are they free,
And I love their great voices,
  Grand and loud as the sea.

In my canopied branches
  Play the things that have wing—
Snugly there do they nestle,
  Snugly there do they sing;
A "Te Deum Laudamus"
  Every morning they say,
And a joyous "Cantata"
  At the close of the day.

My tree-shafts often sparkle
  With the scales of the fold
Of a serpent's rich lustre,
  Shot with azure and gold—
It festoons my high arches
  With its cold snaky wreath,
Or creeps down in my bracken,
  Darkly hiding beneath.

Like the hart of Mæandros
  Flying swift from the cry
Of the hounds of Diana
  When their quarry they spy,
The gaunt wolves of the mountains,
  The wild bull in my bounds,
Madly tore through my thickets
  From the yell of the hounds.

Then the shouts of the hunters,
  And the blasts of the horns,
And the whizzing of javelins
  At the boars and the fawns—
Then the dogs in full cry,
  And hard panting for breath,
Made my forest a chaos
  Of commotion and death.

In my gloomiest recesses,
  Though no spectres may hide,
Some have vouched to have witnessed
  Shadowy spectres to glide;

At the awe of their presence,
  Filled as children with fright,
They have fled from the terrors
  Of such mysteries of night.

Fair and graceful the Dryads
  The mythologist sees,
Lovely nymphs of my bowers
  That enshrine in my trees—
So the pools from my fountains
  With fair Naiads he fills,
Young and beautiful virgins
  Fresh and pure as the rills.

I respond with true echo
  The loud woodpecker's cry,
And the note of the eagle
  Uttered down from the sky;
The king-vulture—fierce tyrant
  Of the valleys below—
Holds his banquet with me,
  His eyes flaring aglow.

I have watchmen in hiding,
  My great grave-hornèd owls,
Whose night-hooting oft startles
  The wild beast as it prowls;
I have eyries, blood-sprinkled,
  Where the young callow brood
Of the falcons are glutted
  With their life-quivering food.

I am proud of my cedars
  Which the ivy entwines,
I am crowned with the plumes
  Of my tall-waving pines;
My thick firs shade a kingdom,
  Massed in power are my elms
O'er the undergrowth-life
  Of my awe-spreading realms.

But my oaks are my glory,
  Grand in strength and in forms;
They have dallied with hurricanes,
  They have played with the storms—
Mocking thunders of centuries,
  They have wrestled with Time,
Waving arms at the lightnings,
  Still they tower up sublime.

I take joy in the cottage
  The lone woodsman may raise,
And the voice of his children
  In my pine-shadowed ways;
While the hermit, lone-brooding
  O'er the ills he has seen,
From the sight of mankind
  In dark umbrage I screen.

Neath the high over-arching,
  Where my boughs spread their tent,
Through my green corridors
  With bright flowrets besprent,

There have sauntered together,
  Where wild goats often browse,
The charmed youth and fair maiden
  Softly whispering their vows.

How is man like the forest,
  With its doves and its snakes,
Its loathed reptiles in ambush,
  The song-thrush in its brakes?
In the depths of his nature
  Subtle serpents may hide;
In the heart of his being
  Love angelic reside.

Song of the Spirit of Beauty.

•   •   •

ON the murmuring brooks I glide,
'Mid the glory of clouds I ride;
Now in a mantle of storm I fly,
Now illuming the earth and sky;
Seen in the gems of the dewy shower,
Seen in the ocean's roll of power,
    My presence is everywhere—
    I am the Daughter of God.

On the wings of the wafting snow,
With their hovering grace I go;
In the morn, with its orient blush,
In the hymns of the woodland bush,
In the tiniest glow-worm's light,
And the sun in his glorious might,
    My presence is everywhere—
    I am the Daughter of God.

In the voice of the whispering breeze,
In the shadows of rocks and trees,
In the eagle's sublimest soar,
And the lion's majestic roar,
In the flower whose perfume tells
Where it hides in secluded dells,
     My presence is everywhere—
     I am the Daughter of God.

I oft coil in the serpent's fold
When it glistens with purple and gold—
In the hues of the stalactite,
As it hangs from its cavern'd height,
In the dome of the starry night,
And the skylark's morning flight,
     My presence is everywhere—
     I am the Daughter of God.

But to woman with charms of Heaven
All my sweetest of beauty is given;
O'er her figure, her motion and face,
Do I shed my most exquisite grace,
And thus crown her earth's loveliest queen,
For nought else e'er so lovely was seen.
     My presence is everywhere—
     I am the Daughter of God.

Song of the Church.

* * *

Since the twilight dawn of Man on earth
    (Revealèd light being dim),
As a mother tends her little ones,
    So I have tended Him
Whom old religions grim or gay
For ages mocked—then—passed away.

When in error's mazes, groping far,
    I came to be his guide,
And to lead him in the "Narrow Way"
    From that which opens wide;
I led him safe through shadows deep,
As shepherds lead their wandering sheep.

I have temples reared through all the earth,
    My holy fonts are there,
And I tend all infants' second birth,
    I lift their hands in prayer;
Baptismal drops, the dews of Heaven,
Through me by men of God are given.

In my courts I often gather them
    At laying on of hands;
Oh, how beautiful such gatherings are—
    How blessed to Christian lauds!
Baptized, confirmed—thus may they then
Grow holy women, holy men.

So, as freshly blooms that bloom of life,
    The love of a loving pair,
At my shrines the marriage tie I seal
    With sacred rites and prayer;
God's blessing on them then shall be
Pronounced by priests of God through *me.*

I have altars to the Holy Christ
    Where'er the sun doth shine,
Where adoring penitents may plead
    The Sacrifice Divine—
Where, from the Atonement for the world
The mystic veil is half unfurl'd.

O'er the earth I spread the Book of God
    Far as the seas can roll,
And its messages of love from Heaven
    I spread from pole to pole;
The Way of Life I thus proclaim
In languages of every name.

To the scenes of grief, to hearts of sorrow,
    I go by night and day,
And I point to where the long to-morrow
    Will wipe all tears away;
To haunts of sin, to homes of woe,
To bless and lift up Christ I go.

When at last life's valley groweth dim,
    Death's gloom fast falling there,
To that valley of awe I quickly come
    With sacrament and prayer;
Thus have I tended millions fled
To the shadow-land of all the dead.

When with grief they bear the dead one home,
    And "earth to earth" is given,
By the open grave, as there they weep,
    I lift their thoughts to Heaven;
For the Holy Watcher in the skies
Shall guard our dust till all shall rise!

Song of the Flowers.

• • •

Sprinkled on earth by fingers above,
　We come, we come with the spring;
Now as the turtle and cuckoo are heard,
　We come, we come as they sing;
Bright as the morning, fresh as the dews,
Sweet is our fragrance, radiant our hues.

Children of Nature, beauty and light,
　We come, the fairest of things—
Pearl'd with the earliest droppings of mist.
　With gems that gleam as a king's;
Children of Nature, of beauty and light,
We come to make Nature more lovely and bright.

Pictured in tapestries, costly and grand,
　We deck the "Chambers of State;"
Woven in coronals, chaplets and wreaths,
　We grace both the lowly and great;
The dwellers in wigwams, in huts, and in towers
All love and delight in the beauty of flowers!

Crowns have their glory—and we, too, have ours,
    In richest magnificence dressed ;
Sweet on the bosom of beauty we shine,
    And bright on the warrior's breast ;
We soften the stone both of altars and tombs,
We breathe all around the sweet breath of our
    blooms.

Sweetening the hands that weave us for thrones,
    Perfuming the steps of the bride,
Garlanding pageants that vanish as dreams,
    Or clouds that melt as they glide—
We thus ever brighten the days that are glad,
And thus ever gladden the days that are sad.

Like to a dial that measures the hours,
    We mark the passing of time ;
Coming in spring with the warbling of birds,
    In summer we glow in our prime ;
But fading with fall of the leaves and the snow,
When winters the blasts of their clarions blow.

Growing on mountains, in garrets and halls,
    In lanes, on banks and by springs,
Blooming 'midst pomp, in casements of slums—
    The cottager's pride and the king's—
We light up the gloom of sad poverty's lot,
And please the sick child as it plays in its cot.

Mighty Immortals are sleeping at rest
   Beneath the fragrance we shed ;
The shrines to their memory are mouldering fast,
   Brief, brief is our stay o'er the dead.
Oft perish their names and are lost, just as we
'Mid changes and death in the whirl of Life's Sea.

Yes—men and their memories flourish as flowers,
   Like flowers how transient they seem !
Life and its sorrows, with love and its joys,
   They come and they go like a dream.
But we come again in the spring as before,
While they come again—never more—never more !

Withering soon, we but blossom to die ;
   We symbol man as he goes—
His days so soon spent, and his strength is soon
     gone,
   When touched by Time as it flows ;
He passes like us, transient flowers of the earth,
Beginning to die on the day of his birth.

To cottage and palace, to valley and mead,
   We come, we come, every year,
To sweeten the homes of the rich and the poor
   When cuckoos and swallows appear ;
As winter departs, we still come again,
Bright types of the grand Resurrection of men.

Bloom then, oh bloom, ye bright flowers of our
        God!
    Bloom on, so loved and so sweet,
Making the world far more beautiful still,
    More fit for saintliest feet!
Bloom on, oh ye fairest, ye loveliest things!
The Muse of creation your loveliness sings.

Love's Own Song.

• • •

MY name is "Love." My songs and power
Are sweet as breath and bloom of flower.
In earth beneath, in Heaven above,
No charm is there like that of love—
Best boon to man that e'er was given,
I come a spirit bright from Heaven,
    To sing around, below, above—
    "No charm is there like that of love!"

To palace-halls I speed my wings,
And rule on thrones in breasts of kings;
The peasant's cot I fill with bliss,
And ball-room beauties love my kiss;
The school-girl feels my kindly glow
As fresh as dew, as pure as snow,
    And softly sings as coo of dove—
    "No charm is there like that of love!

The soldier's sword he wields for me,
The sailor woos me o'er the sea;
Enchanting on the stage I seem
As fondest things of poet's dream;
I weave the brightest spells of life
Around the husband and the wife,
　　Who both may sing—" All things above,
　　No bliss is there like that of love!"

Song of Death.

• • •

I SOLVE not the groping Reasoner's guess
  Of *what* I am or why—
I show not the "dark beyond" as yet,
  Though "it" is ever nigh;
I open my dusky gate each day
For all that in thousands pass away.

My mystical shadows, dark and deep,
  I may not yet dispel,
Nor what the departed know and feel
  Can I to mortals tell;
My mission is done when I translate
The spirit of men to the " After State.

Deep down in the ground where earthquakes closed
  Lies many a mouldering head—
Embedded in sands—enshrined in rocks,
  I hide some ancient dead;
No marble or bronze e'er marked the spot
Where, sleeping through ages, they sleep forgot.

Where navies their broadside thunders hurl
　　And dauntless heroes slay,
Where armies their battle-revels hold,
　　I hover o'er the fray;
Where red is the grass and red the wave
I hover as sink and fall the brave.

In ivory homes though men may dwell,
　　Ablaze with gorgeous show,
Though grim is my portal, yet at last
　　Through *this* they all must go,
And sleep in the realm of darkest shade,
Where myriads of earth's past dead are laid.

Till closed is the last of human graves
　　I knock at every door,
And seize in their turn all those within,
　　Who *then* return no more;
For, laid in the dust of holy ground,
They slumber with me till judgment sound.

I empty the homes and thrones of kings—
　　And every donjon-keep;
I empty the cradles where the pets
　　Of loving mothers sleep;
I empty all seats of power and pride
And snatch from her bliss the blooming bride.

I come for the *child* of radiant locks,
     And *shall* do through all time;
I come for the *youth*, all fresh in life,
     For *man* in fullest prime;
I come where the poor in squalor pine,
As well as where pomps of grandeur shine.

The head that is sad I lay to rest,
     I still the troubled heart,
The fluttering fears of every breast
     At my cold touch depart;
I dry up the tears that mourners pour,
Who rest where I come and weep no more.

'Tis only through *me* the saints can reach
     Their home in Heavenly Light—
Through me in their woe the lost must go
     To everlasting Night;
I usher them both to where their lot,
Or woeful or blissful, altereth not.

Once, life from the "Lord of Life" I took,
     But *back* to life He woke—
My bars and my bands, tho' thought so strong,
     As withered withs He broke;
So He, by the death of *Death*, shall be
O'er death and the grave, "the victory."

Ibunger Personified.

• • •

I AM supreme o'er nature's orb,
  The sovereign mover there,
Urging to action every life
  In water, earth or air :
Tiniest things in their dewdrop-homes
  No less than mightiest whales,
Creatures that swim, or fly, or creep—
  On all my power prevails.

Forced by an impulse given by me,
  The mighty lions prowl,
Shaking the rustling jungles dense
  That swell the echoing howl ;
Wolves in their packs I fiercely lash
  Swift down the mountain side,
Which to escape, with precious life,
  Swift must the horseman ride.

Down from his height the eagle swoops
  When goaded sharp by me ;
Down I descend and wield my power
  In depths of every sea—

Banqueting there on maidens fair,
  Deep in the watery dark,
Raving and pitiless, I send
  The dread devouring shark.

Buccaneers and bandits wild
  I make as fierce as free,
The savage in his savage haunts
  Is savage made by me;
Men in their masses, reft of food,
  I rouse to frenzied strife—
To barricades and wreck and fire
  And holocausts of life.

This is my *wilder* work and force;
  My *common* sway is mild,
Gentle as gentlest meek desire
  Of even a little child;
Pleasant the zest of luscious fruits,
  That zest is born of me,
Who in my purpose, under God,
  Am God's wise mystery.

PART IV.

• • •

A Tale in Verse.

The Hop-picker.

* * *

THE verandah, all blooms, cast a cool chequered shade,
And beneath it oft seen was a bright cottage maid;
Very lovely her figure, her eyes, and her hair,
Sweetly simple of speech, sweetly guileless and fair;
Hence the handsome young Squire from the hall which
    was nigh,
Without errand or mission would often pass by.
Day by day he would pause through the bushes to peep,
But at times to her side he would daintily creep,
And incline o'er her form, draped in unsullied white,
While the jasmines were waving to toy with the light.
To his soft wooing whisper she whispered again:
" By your love I am flattered—yet to love me is vain;
Though 'twere rapture to me if I *could* but be thine,
Yet an honour so brilliant can never be mine.
You might claim with acceptance the white jewelled
    hand
Of a high stately heiress, the belle of the land,
But for *me*, of so simple and lowly estate,
You are far, far too noble—too grand and too great."

" Not of high mountain flowers do I most love the grace,
But the *wee* one, the *sweet* one, that blooms at its base."

This he said, when her brow, which was pure as the snow,
With the peach's soft blush began faintly to glow—
For a cottager's daughter to wed with the Squire—
What a theme for the gossips as they sit by their fire !

" All of rank," she made answer, "your mansion would
　　flee,
And with scorn turn their backs both on you and on me.
No, no ! *never* for *me* shall you forfeit a friend,
So, it grieves me to say it, our meetings must end ;
Let our farewell be *now*—now our saddest good-night,
Though the joy of these hours fills my heart with delight.
May no cloud ever darken the sun of your life,
Though I share not its light as your much-honoured wife !
Let us part, not to meet—but yet still, I must own,
How I loved you and prized the fond hours that have
　　flown."

　　　　　　At the hop-picking season
　　　　　　She went with the shoals
　　　　　That were swarming to gather
　　　　　The leaf from the poles.

As so deftly her fingers were picking for days,
There were many that stood on her beauty to gaze,
And amongst them a youth—such a bright gallant swain—
But with garments much torn and much mended again ;

Rather golden his beard, rather shaggy his brows—
Rather heavy his boots, and much faded his blouse ;
On his hat the night-fellows their larks had begun,
And had kicked it about in their frenzy of fun.

To the cottager's daughter
He opened his plaint,
And his brogue was so winsome,
So sparkling, so quaint !

Much she liked what he said in a bright magic style ;
There was love in his voice—there was love in his smile ;
While around him there floated—but what ?—could she
tell ?—
'Twas the mystery that thrills through the heart like a
spell.
As his clothes he excused, she assured him, with reason,
They were quite good enough for the hop-picking
season,
Though she modestly shrank to be heard or be seen
Tête-à-tête with a youth in so tattered a mien.
She replied when at last the soft question he pressed :
" Yes, I *would*—but for *one,* above *all* I love best—

The good Squire, near my home, who is all to my
mind,
But his love and his offer *with grief* I declined :
For I felt that a girl of so humble a grade
Was unfit for the pomps in his mansion displayed—

That the ladies so stately, so proud, and high-born,
In the blaze of their grandeur would shame me to scorn.
Can you take then a heart to *another* that's given,
Whom I *never* can wed, though to wed him were Heaven ?
If you can, I am yours—you I *could* not refuse,
For of all, next to *him, you* I only would choose."

        His emotions of rapture—
          What pen could define !
        As he clasped her, exclaiming—
          "At last you are mine !"

Now, as homeward they wended and settled the day,
Softly fluttered her heart, and her spirits were gay.
To her cottage she went; the verandah, her shade,
Was a screen from the sun to the sweet cottage-maid,
And as *there* she sat dreaming the dreams of a bride,
Lo ! the hop-picking youth stood again by her side;
But how changed was his mien—how changed his attire !
For the hop-picking youth was her lover—the Squire.
Not now golden his beard, and not shaggy his brows,
Not now quaint was his brogue, and not faded his blouse;
The young lord of the mansion had doffed his disguise,
And revealed his true self to her wondering eyes.

Who can tell what the word she will say to him now ?
She had *sworn* to be his—she will *keep* to her *vow;*
He had bowed to her state—in disguise won her heart,
She will *cling* to him now, nor till death wish to part.

> Thus her loveliness triumphed,
>   His gallantry too,
> And their love-test was proof
> Each to other was true !

When the flowerets should bloom with the next coming
      spring,
They arranged for the wedding, the robes, and the ring—
That her dress should be chaste, not too grand, not too
      loud,
But as white as the drifts of a white-woven cloud ;
And as gold needs no gilding, no gems would she wear,
Not a brilliant or pearl, though he brought the most rare.
No—the jewels she chose for her glad marriage-hour,
Were the *beauty God gave* and a sweet orange-flower.
When the wedding-morn broke there was pealing of bells,
And the trooping with roses of fair village-girls.

Now the bride, with a smile on her beautiful face,
From her cottage glides forth like a vision of grace,
While the throngs of the villagers, heading the choir,
Fill the air with their cheers for the maiden and Squire.
Under garlands they go to the church close at hand—
She of figure so light, he of manhood so grand.

By the altar within ne'er before had there been
Such a mingling of ranks or a happier scene.
There were women in costumes, poor, homely, and plain;
Their were ladies and peasants, the shepherd and swain ;

Then a band of rich maidens, in draperies of snow,
Stood in white silken zones with pure lilies in blow ;
For so spotless the fame, so enchanting the bride,
That the *hauteur* of rank sank its scorn at her side.

When the service was done,
On his arm she came forth,
A most beautiful bride,
Like an angel on earth.

Over blossoms and carpets they enter the hall,
Where her life in a cottage she would often recall.
There the gay festal-board with profusion was crowned,
There the toasts and good wishes re-echoed around ;
Then the blessings of earth, with the blessings of
Heaven,
Were invoked from on high on the pair to be given ;
While *without* there was ringing "God bless them !"
aloud,
In the heartiest cheers from the jubilant crowd.

Then the bells join their voices with far-sounding peals,
Loudly spreading the gladness o'er hamlets and fields,
While the children with garlands, their gift to the
bride,
Lift their voices with joy and are heard far and wide.
They come smiling and cheering — a bright gleeful
throng—
They come smiling and cheering and singing this song :—

THE CHILDREN'S SONG.

" Hand-in-hand, all joined together,
    Dancing on your velvet lawn,
We, though only little children,
    Come to hail your wedding morn.
Cheering, dancing, clapping, prancing—
    Bounding—leaping like a fawn !

" We were at the church this morning,
    And we saw how blessed you were ;
Golden was the benediction
    Which for you we sought in prayer.
Dancing lightly, smiling brightly,
    Now our cheers shall fill the air.

" May your days be bright and joyous—
    Joyous as we children are—
Sunshine playing o'er you ever,
    Each to each life's sweetest star !
Singing, skipping, lightly tripping,
    Glad—how glad—we children are !

" Hand-in-hand, all joined together,
    Here we hail the fairy bride,
And the bridegroom, tall and handsome,
    There so happy at her side !
Merry, blessing, fond, caressing,
    May your lives as music glide !"

When the singing was ended, the bridegroom appears
To acknowledge the plaudits, the clapping and cheers,
There was *one*, far the tiniest of that happy band,
Crowned with tresses of gold, with a flower in her hand,
And he raised her and tossed her, and said in his glee—
As a gift from me, Bonny, say what shall it be?

> " Gif me, p'ease, a softy kiss,
> Then I glad will gif you this—(the flower);
> I would like a goldy pear,
> And a lock of Bridy's hair,
> Which I'll keep for efermore,
> Here inside my pinafore;
> And, sir, mudder tell me say—
> Wis' you happy mar-idge-day,
> Tzat what mudder tell me say."

Then with echoes tumultuous and swelling on high,
All the children responded, electric with joy :—

> " Yes, sir, don't be long away,
> That's what *all* we children say—
> Hip, hip, we'll shout!—Hip, hip, hoora!
> Louder still!—Hoora! hoora!"

Fast the moments are speeding, and he watches the time
To depart with his bride for a sunnier clime;
But, ere then, he proclaims from the steps of the hall,
That the day must be kept as a high festival.

In his park 'neath the shade of a giant oak tree,
Was a banquet prepared in a stately marquee ;
Then a welcome is bid (for his bride so desires)
To the young men and maidens, the matrons and sires.
" To the children," he said, " the bright loved ones of
    Heaven,
Do we wish some choice things of the feast to be
    given ;
And forget not to toast, in a bumper's full tide,
The fair Queen of my home—my dear beautiful Bride.
But our carriage is near, so a transient farewell,
Come, be all of you merry—Farewell and Farewell !"

Now depart the happy pair,
Followed by the village-prayer,
And the cheers of boys and girls,
And the pealing of the bells—
    Clapping, clanging, dong, ding-dong !

Far those cheers of gladness fly,
Merrily echoing through the sky ;
Far is heard the belfry song
Raised by ringers, loud and long—
    Clapping, clanging, dong, ding-dong !

Bells, those bells !—their thrilling sound
Gladdens all the homes around ;
Park and valley speed along
Echoes of their bridal song—
    Clapping, clanging, dong, ding-dong !

> Crowds of village forms there press
> Lovingly the pair to bless,
> And they sing the song of glee
> With the bell-tower's melody—
> 　Clapping, clanging, dong, ding-dong!

Far away did he take her from scenes of her birth
To the scenes and the cities—the grandest of earth,
Where cathedrals that echoed with anthems divine
Were emblazoned with monument, altar and shrine;
And he took her to castles long mem'ried in story—
To saloons of high pomp, and to gardens of glory;
To the palaces famed as the home of great kings;
To old ruins where the ivy of centuries clings;
And to theatres glittering with fashion's bright throng,
Where were beauty and brightness and dancing and
　　song.
Here, she heard the loud plashing of fountains that
　　played—
There, the sound of the fall of the rushing cascade.
Arm-in-arm would they watch the processions of nuns,
As in white they oft walked where the gilded stream runs.
To their chantings so holy, 'mid shrubberies and flowers,
Would they listen secluded in fairy-like bowers.
When the moon silvered o'er the calm face of the sea,
Then its ripples to them full of music would be;
But at last, as they sat on a rock by the shore,
They resolved their long wanderings now should be o'er.
Her white arm on his shoulder, her eyes on his face,
She quite dazzled his heart with her beautiful grace.

  " My own loved one," she said,
   " Since you first became mine,
  You have brightened my life,
   As light brightens a shrine.

A new freshness seems *now* upon all things around,
From the blue of the sky to the green of the ground;
When with *you*, how much lovelier the songs of the
   wood !
When with *you*, how much deeper my wish to be good !
Though enchanting the things which with you I have seen,
Yet *far dearer* than all to my heart *you have been.*
Oh, your love is to me the best flower under Heaven,
And yourself the best gift which to me God has given !
As we cease in these lands any longer to roam,
I must soon take my place in your beautiful home;
But my little heart fears I may not do it well,
As you have raised me so high from a coy cottage girl.
But I know, my own loved one, whatever betide,
Will the bliss of your presence be still by my side.
How I hope to be ever the joy of your life,
And to honour your house in my sphere as your wife—
That you *will* not be spurned for my lowly estate,
Since our bridal was honoured by humble and great.
To the poor all around I shall wish to be kind,
To be meek in my splendour, and as light to the blind :
To the beds of the sick will you, dear, let me go,
And to those who by troubles are sorely brought low ?
And to chambers of anguish and quivering breath,
May I go to console where there is mourning and death ?"

As she uttered these words,
An ethereal light
Softly swept o'er her features
So blooming and bright.

All encircled she seemed with a beauty so sweet,
That the haughtiest pride softened down at her feet.
"Yes, oh yes!" he replied—"not a wish you could name
But is sacred to me as is love's holy flame.
You the sunshine will be of my years yet to come,
The sweet minist'ring angel to brighten my home.
To fulfil all your wishes as we journey through life,
Will be dear to me ever, my darling, my wife!"

Now the homeward return is resolved on at last,
But what sights and what scenes have *again* to be passed!
Lands of lakes and of vineyards, of pomegranate shades;
Lands of cedars and palms and of orange arcades.
O'er the sea that on earth through all ages hath roamed,
And through States richly citied and towered and domed,
To their home (as their journey is nearing its end)
Do these long-travelled pilgrims a courier send,
With the tidings that ere the next evening is o'er,
They will be in their dear native village once more.

Ere they *see* in the distance the village church rise,
Do they *hear* its bells peal through the echoing skies—
Now as music they sound, *now* sonorous their clangs;
Now so soft are their chimes, *now* so mighty their bangs.

By the time (rushing on) their proud horses are seen,
The whole village, to greet them, is massed on the green:
There they pause, while some groups, filing out from
    the crowd,
Thus with glad salutations address them aloud :—

OLD MEN AND MATRONS.

" Though *we* are old, with shaky voices,
    And near the end of life's long track,
    Yet *you* we come, with feeble footsteps,
    To cheer, and hail, and welcome back !"

YOUNG MEN AND MAIDENS.

" Oh ! lightly and brightly, with gladsomest song,
    To welcome you back, we come marching along ;
        So gladly appearing,
        With jubilant cheering,
To meet you and greet you, we hasten, we throng !"

LITTLE CHILDREN.

" Oh ! happy bridegroom, welcome home,
    And you, his pretty bride !
We little ones, to greet you back,
    Have hastened to your side.
Please accept this gift of ours—
This, a simple gift of flowers ;
Some that bloomed beside the brooks,
Some that blushed in woodland nooks—

                        G

Water-lilies and wild roses
Woven into wreaths and posies;
While they sparkled bright with dew,
Then we culled them all for you!"

TINY AGAIN,

Held by her Mother's hand.

" I so like come in your car-idge,
    And to kiss you for your mar-idge;
I so like sit on your knee
To hear you tell you lovey me.
Here I'fe got my little dolly
Which we kisten 'Pretty Polly;'
I will lend it you to play,
Always on your mar-idge day;
I so merry 'gain to see
You com'd back akoss the sea!"

When the greetings were o'er, and responses were made,
Then the proud horses pranced round the old garden
        glade;
'Neath the patriarch-oaks and the bronze massive gates,
Do they reach the old hall where a smiling group
        waits.
Had the cottage sylph been of high-honoured grade,
Of a lineage in grandest escutcheons displayed,
Not more cheery her welcome to home could have been,
For the joy in the hall equalled that on the green.

At a banquet soon given to a festival throng,
There were gay gliding dancers, and daughters of song;
There were beauties among them—bright stars of the
    ball,
But the *bride* was more beautiful *far* than they all.

．　　　．　　　．　　　．　　　．　　　．　　　．　　　．　　　．

In the midst of the dance and the songs of the fête
Comes the sound of the rolling of wheels to the gate;
Then a ring at the door, where a Gypsy crone stands—
Black as raven's her hair, brown and withered her hands;
There were rents in her garments unlooped to the winds,
And her thin withered visage was furrowed with lines.

Harsh and husky her voice, weird and haggard her look,
Cold as steel flashed her eyes, and her palsied frame shook;
She had nothing to beg, she had nothing to sell,
But a secret of *years* to the Master to tell.

With the bride and the bridegroom, to look at the sight,
Trips a group of young belles—all as fairies in white;
The gaunt dame to the beauties all round bowed her head,
And at last in the hall, lowly curtseying, said:—

．　　　．　　　．　　　．　　　．　　　．　　　．　　　．

    " I come, Sir, though so lank and old,
      My visage tinged like yellow mould—
      I come, a mystery to reveal,
      A secret I'll no more conceal:

Don't start so, ladies, though I'm grim—
So crook'd of back, deformed of limb;
Don't shrink and look so stark amazed—
I'm not a witch, nor am I crazed;
No spells of sorceress have I brought,
And by no spells am I distraught;
Though grimly spectral I appear,
I come to speak with Master here!

.　　.　　.　　.　　.　　.　　.

" Oh, Sir! *great Sir*, your youthful bride,
So like an angel by your side
(If here to tell it I am free),
Is not what she is *thought* to be.
On tramp, a roving Gypsy wild
(When she was but a little child),
I passed the burnished gates of one
Whose castle-towers, high gleaming, shone:
The child—a little thing of joy—
Came toddling through as I passed by;
Her nurse had gone, as I suppose,
To pluck herself a gaudy rose;
I took the child, as there it stood,
And plunged into the neighbouring wood;
In caverns there, all through the night
I hid, with qualms and full of fright.
Next morn I tramped, and tramped for days
Through dark and twisting, winding ways;
My mazy course I still held on,
Till weary weeks and months had gone.

Her clothes, the grandest I had seen,
Would suit the nursery of a queen;
I sold them, in repentant mood,
To buy ourselves a little food.
Its coral rattle I have kept,
Which long it played with—with it slept,
And in its bodice was imprest
The great grand Earl's armorial crest—
That, too, I kept, and have it here
In this rag, folded many a year.
I loved the child with rough delight,
It was so pretty, good, and bright;
The smoky camp, hence far away,
Was happier for its smiles and play;
On straw it laid its little head,
And straw was then its only bed.

.   .   .   .

" One night a priest came with his lamp,
To speak of Jesus in the camp;
And, though from this hard breast no prayer
E'er rose to God up yonder there,
For one to teach the *child* to pray,
I much had longed from day to day.
The priest, a kind, good, holy man
(As towards him, o'er the straw she ran),
Embraced and kissed her; and I said,
While tears down these lank cheeks were shed,
' Oh, teach her words to say to God,
As on our weary way we plod !'

Then, kneeling on the straw spread there
He raised her hands for solemn prayer,
And said, 'My sweet one, on your knee,
Look up to God and say with me.'
How softly echoed through the brake
Her pretty utterings as she spake!
This was the prayer which, after him,
She said beside his lamp-light dim;
With joy, my old heart fluttered then
And, at the end, I said, 'Amen!'

The Prayer.

' My Jesus, in Thy garden,
   I'm but a tiny flower,
  Oh, tend me, guard me, bless me,
   Each day, each night, each hour!

' When winds the camp are shaking,
   And *on* it fall the rains,
  When we are camping nightly
   In long and lonely lanes,
  Oh, guard us as on earth we lie,
   And be Thou, Saviour, ever nigh!

' And bless the loving Gypsy,
   Who makes me all her care;
  Please fill her heart with comfort,
   With love of Thee and prayer;

'And if I have a father,
  Let me my father see;
And if I have a mother,
  Oh, lead me to her knee!

' Here *on* me *be* Thy sunshine,
  And *round* me be Thy arms,
Till, up to Heaven Thou take me—
  To its golden harps and palms!

'My Jesus, in Thy garden,
  I'm but a tiny flower,
Please tend me, guard me, bless me,
  Each day, each night, each hour!'

Full many a time, as on we strolled
Through winding ways and wood and wold,
That prayer was said at fall of night,
And at the rise of morning light.

.   .   .   .

" At last my conscience drove me wild
For stealing such a high-born child,
From such a glorious castle-home,
With me, a Gypsy, far to roam.
No matter where or what my track,
My conscience whispered: 'Take her back!'
But this I feared, lest I should be
Deprived of my wild liberty.
What plans I formed! what schemes I drew!
My mind was harassed what to do.

O'er many a hill and many a plain,
By many a cross-road—many a lane,
I wandered, wandered—weary, weary,
And all my path seemed dark and dreary;
The little child by hand I led,
Sweet sunshine of the course we sped.

. . . .

" Though long she had not learned to walk,
And only lately learned to talk,
Her pretty prattle, all day long,
To me was like a lovely song.
She loved to gather road-side flowers,
And see the rainbow in the showers,
The smoke far twirling down the breeze,
The squirrels leaping in the trees—
To see the weasel, hare and stoat,
And golden clouds in glory float—
To gaze at gaudy butterflies,
And larks high soaring in the skies;
Her nature mingled with delight
With every joyous sound and sight.

. . . . . .

" We called at mansions, villas, farms,
To seek for refuge, milk, or alms;
The child's rich golden beauty bright—
Sweet thing of loveliness and light

(O'er which I'd cast a bane—a curse)—
Unlocked each heart—if not each purse,
And won us many a cosy rest
On beds of straw her prayers blessed.

.   .   .   .

" One eve our course, with wearied pace,
Led near *this hall*—this joyous place ;
I brought the child across the moor
And took her to the cottage door—
The cottage, with white creepers flowered,
Verandah'd, trellised, ivied, bowered.
I *left* her for the dame to mind
While I came *here*,—'twas but a *blind;*
I went not *back*, nor ventured *here*,
I fluttered so with guilty fear ;
For conscience smites, with equal stings,
The breasts of gypsies and of kings.

.   .   .   .

" Since then—'tis seventeen years ago—
I've tramped and wandered to and fro ;
In all my camping, everywhere,
I've nursed her priest-taught little prayer,
And felt how deep in crime I fell
To kidnap such an angel-girl ;
No grief e'er tore a woman's heart
Like mine from her at last to part—
To part from all that clung to me
Of that sweet child's sweet memory !

.   .   .   .

" Now, Sir, at this gay festal fête,
　Though these rent rags reveal my state,
　I come to crown your married life
　By telling you *that child's your wife!*
　No humble cotter's birth had she,
　But one of high nobility,
　The daughter of a Hero-Earl,
　Whose castle-banners high unfurl,
　In whose bright halls was weeping wild
　When I had stolen his heiress-child.

　　.　　.　　.　　.　　.　　.　　.

" Ere to my camp again I stray,
　Full many a hundred miles away,
　I leave her bodice with its crest
　Her true identity to test;
　Her coral-rattle, too, I show
　As further proof before I go.

　　.　　.　　.　　.　　.　　.

" But will you deign, dear gracious ma'am,
　To show us all your right-hand palm?
　I feel I can't mistaken be,
　Though not professing palmistry.
　Have you a cross, cut there one day
　As on your castle-walls you lay,
　A cross upon the line of life?—
　Best sign to grace a happy wife?"

　　.　　.　　.　　.　　.　　.　　.

All looked, and lo! the cross was there—
Cross ever lifted at her prayer,
More precious gem than could be set
In any earl's rich coronet!

.   .   .   .

With salaams quaint and gifts not few,
The mystic Gypsy then withdrew.

.   .   .   .

Then again came the rolling of wheels to the hall,
A pageant emblazoned more than wont for a ball.
"Rat-at-tat!" went the knocker, loud sounded the bell—
A distinguished arrival all knew it did tell.
Through the door as it opened there was given the
    name,
"Earl and Countess de Vaux,"—not unhonoured of fame.
From the dance, briefly resting, was standing the Bride
In the hall of reception—the Squire by her side;
With their high, stately guests all due forms were
    exchanged,
And a short *tête-à-tête* was politely arranged.

.   .   .   .

THE EARL—

"We lost our daughter many years ago,
Our only child and heiress—crushing blow!
Sad by our fire, long, long we sat and waited
For her dear footsteps, till we deemed it fated

That we, bereft, our child should see no more
Come toddling towards us through the opening door.
That watching, waiting—oh, our hopeless state!
Now seeking early, and now seeking late.
Our castle lost its joy, our hearth its light,
When she was gone, so pretty and so bright.
A Gypsy crone—three hundred miles away—
Sent word she knew where once it used to stay.
We sent her money, sent a pleading guest,
To come at once and set our hearts at rest.
She came, she said 'twas in a cottage here,
Which she could show us if we brought her near.
My castle-home stands at a distance far,
A two days' journey from the ocean-bar.
We posted here, impatient of delay,
And brought the Gypsy with us all the way.
We reached the little cottage, where she said
The dame knew all—alas! the dame was dead!
A maid there cried (she made our spirits glow)—
'The Squire can tell you all you wish to know.'
At once we drove the Gypsy to your door,
That you and she might talk the mystery o'er.
Now *she* is gone, we come *ourselves* to see
What trace of her, if any, here may be."

.   .   .   .

THE SQUIRE—

" She says *she stole* the child and, forced to fly—
Last left it at the cottage here hard by.

See—here's a coral rattle which she brought,
The name 'de Vaux' upon it plainly wrought;
And here's a bodice, broidered and imprest
With these initials, coronet and crest."

.   .   .   .

With a look at these things what a change, what a sight!
For the Countess swooned down like a star of the night,
The bloom fled from her cheek and the light from her eye,
And her colourless lips could not utter a cry;
As a candle blown out, seemed her life to have fled,
And her forehead was blanched as the brow of the dead.
But ere long there was motion, faint tremor, and sighs,
And at last the slow opening of lips and her eyes.
When to life fresh and conscious, again she awoke,
Seizing rattle and bodice, she clasped them and spoke.

THE COUNTESS—

" Oh lost one, dear one, this was thine!—
    This rattle in thy little hand,
    Tied round thy waist with silken band
    And silvery bells, ere thou couldst stand—
Oh, lost one, dear one, this was thine!

    " In the ivory handle here I see
    The two initals 'H' and 'G,'
    'Hilda,' 'Gladys,' cut for thee;
    And here, this coronet and crest,
    With magic power my eyes arrest,

What sorrows, too, are linked with all !
 With my own hands I stamped them here ;
 Since *then* I've shed the bitter tear
 Through many a long ungladdened year.
What joys these little things recall !

" Oh, perished days ! oh, perished days !
When I so loved her little ways,
Her patter, clatter, laugh, and gaze !
What memories wake and round them cling—
What griefs to me those memories bring !
But if, by means I know not how,
My child *could* stand before me *now*,
A 'child' she *would* not, *could* not be,
But 'woman' grown, not knowing me,
 Yet still a child, *my* child to me !
How, how to find her . . . would we knew !
Oh, that we had some guiding clue !"

 . . . .

THE SQUIRE—

" *Madam*, I might by *dearer* name than *this*
Accost you in my overflow of bliss.
I have a clue, a *clear* one—yes, and more,
A *proof* transcending any lawyer's lore.
Yes, proof on proof that Gypsy has revealed,
Though kept by her for years on years concealed.
She pointed out the cottage at whose door
She left your daughter seventeen years before ;

She brought the coral rattle with its bells;
(And what a tale that little trinket tells!)
She found it on her when she stole your child—
A deed she mourns with grimmest grief and wild.
The initials, mark, the coronet and crest—
She showed them all, your daughter to attest,
And prove her yours—henceforth a mother blest!

   .   .   .   .

" And *now behold this lady* by my side—
My home-star, loved one, angel, bride!
She, she's your child, your lost one, found at last!
Who hence will tell you all her history past."

   .   .   .   .

Then what gushing of heart in the scene now
    appears!
What embracings and claspings, what kisses and
    tears!
With their arms round the neck of each other
    entwined,
And their hands firmly grasped in their rapture of
    mind.
With their joy overwrought at the lost being found,
How their broken and fond exclamations resound!
Like the waves of the sea rolling bright to the shore,
Swell the waves of emotion at meeting once more.

THE COUNTESS—

" My daughter! Hilda. . . . Gladys! Yes!
    It is, it is, my own—my own!
Yes! here's the cross cut when you fell,
A charming little *Infant Belle.*
    But *now* . . . a lovely *Woman* grown.
My daughter—long-lost daughter—yes!
    It is, it is, my own—my own!

   .   .   .   .

" Oh, dark and sad have been the days
    Since you were kidnapped from your home—
Too young to tell whose child you were,
Too young to say an infant's prayer.
    My lamb long stolen, far to roam,
But *now* at last come home—come home!
    My long-lost child, my own—my own!"

   .   .   .   .

THE BRIDE—

" My father! My mother!
    Oh, those words,
    How sweet—how dear!
How strangely from my lips they fall!
And not till *now*, till in this hall,
    Have I so called you.

Transported with delight new found,
How passing dear to me they sound!
How all my nature thrills and glows
At words so dear, so sweet as those.

  .   .   .   .

" When cradled in the Gypsy's camp I lay,
She asked a priest to teach me how to pray.
The night was dark, the stars were twinkling round;
He had a lamp, and knelt upon the ground,
His visage gleaming with the light he brought.
This is the prayer my infant mind he taught—

    ' If now I have a *father*,
       Let me my father see;
    And if I have a *mother*,
       Oh, lead me to her knee!'

He taught me *more*, all which I have forgot;
But *this* from memory nought can *ever* blot.
This prayer is heard, my *father* here I see,
And here I stand beside my *mother's* knee!

  .   .   .   .

  " Events and times, how fast they glide!
    For, when by you last seen,
  I was a *babe* . . . but now a bride—
    What span of years between!

  .   .   .   .

H

" My husband here—
Yes, this is he,
My choice of all earth's family—
He did not scorn
To note my cot,
And raise me to a statelier lot.
His pride he stooped
To honour me,
And lavish love's sweet ministry:
Of manly heart,
Of noble worth,
No dearer bridegroom on the earth !

 . . . .

" Our wedding fêtes are scarcely done,
Our wedded home-life scarce begun—
This night, in his ancestral hall,
We celebrate this nuptial ball.
Oh father ! mother !—sacred sound ! -
What joy that I, your lost, am found !
How strange the chance that ·you should be
At this our bright festivity !"

Thus the hop-picker bride Lady Hilda became,
And most sweetly she graced her position and name ;
Not the lamb on the lawn, not a child in its glee,
Not a being on earth, was more happy than she.

PART V.

• • •

Miscellaneous Poems.

A Throng of Mountains:

THEIR GLORIOUS GRANDEUR.

* * *

BENEATH their shadow slept a peaceful lake.
To soothe and so forget his many griefs,
A youthful genius, sad with shattered hopes,
Here paddled on to scan the towering rocks.
Full soon his oar-plash ceased its rippling sound,
And awe and wonder filled his brooding heart
As round him clustering rose the Mountain-Throng.

" Ye ancient hills" (he said), "majestic thrones
Of the great thunder, voiceless, yet your speech
Has mingled with the sound of ages gone.
When, warm and glowing from the hand of God,
The young sun slanted his first morning-light,

And gilded your proud coronets of mist,
How fresh were *ye!* How beautiful was *he!*
As bright and fadeless is he now as then ;
And so are ye that wear not yet the blanch
Of the hoary power erst bid to spare but sea
And earth, the stars and ever youthful sky,
But chartered oft to bleach the locks, and steal
Their loveliness from earth's most lovely ones,
And sprinkle them with grave-dust ! '*Me*, ah *me!*
Ye mock ! Let dawn a few more morrows here,
And I shall sleep beneath the grass.'" As flowers
That speak the sweetest language of the ground
A little while, *then* strew their shrivelled leaves
Around our footsteps, echoing as we stray
The crisp, low rustlings of mortality—
So his young spirit, full of promise once
As any flower that ever bloomed in spring,
Shrank brooding on the change to be his lot.

Before the genius of eternal youth
That lived enshrined in the agèd hills, he felt
His life was as the shadow of a cloud.
He listlessly his oar then plied again,
And roamed, he recked not whither. Soon a scene
Of battered vastness—mountains, scathed and rived,
Broke on his eye ! There broke, too, on his heart
The dread Divinity of the mighty scenes.
With awe he scanned these pinnacles of power,
The solemn shade of whose immensity
Slanted afar, and filled the air with gloom.

" Ha ! ha !" (he said) " ye thunder-cloven crags,
That drip with breath of Old Eternity,
I feel the awe of your great agèdness !
E'en ye, so huge and mighty, cannot hide
Your overwhelm of unrecorded years !
In furrowed hieroglyphs the hand of Time
Has graved the tale of storms upon your brows,
And wrinkled you with venerable scars !
The lightnings of his thousand years have spent
Their revelry of wild omnipotence
Upon your heights. And though vast ancient lakes
Have hourly bathed your feet for ages past,
And though soft dews, bright tear-drops of the
     sky,
So long have trickled down the quiet air,
And pearl'd your tow'ring forms, yet vain—*all*
     vain—
No greenness clothes you with its youthful hue,
The valley's livery. Round your hoary heads
The twilight of eternal evening falls,
While down your chasm'd hearts a darkness dwells
As deep as that which covers with its pall
Th' unstoried mockeries of things gone by !
Such darkness soon will overspread us all,
And we shall vanish as our fathers did—
Their final farewells followed by our own."

A farewell, too, he thought of as he rowed,
And hummed it to a melancholy air,
In rhythm with his oars. These were the words—

" Farewell is the word of all nature,
    The *breeze*, as it flows through the dell,
The *brook* and the *cloud* and the *shadow*,
    As onward they pass, say ' Farewell ! '

" The joys that *have been* and departed,
    The hopes that arose and then fell—
Memorials, perished forever,
    Are linked with some bygone farewell.

" But who of our fondest and dearest
    The sorrowful feelings could tell,
When parting, *they*, too, had to say
    The last and the saddest farewell ? "

Flung in wild masses down the channelled rocks
From grand and dizzy loftiness, he saw
The silver gush of echoing waters leap.
Prone down in everlasting shadows whelmed,
He watched their fall, and thus in thought exclaimed—

" Oh beautiful, ye streams !—*how* beautiful,
    Ye cataracts of light ! With diamond gleams
    Your gushing glory bursts from cavern'd glooms
    Swift into the air of light ! 'Tis thus that man,
    Undarkened by the shadow of the grave,
    Shall spring again to life—a spirit bright,
    And not as ye, to fall engulfed below,
    But *higher* still to *rise*, and brighter glow
    Nearer and nearer still to God in Heaven."

But Evening now,

That sweetest smile of the great sky,
Came down. Forth, grained with amethyst and gold,
The huge rock-walls were 'sprent with water-gems;
A thousand, thousand golden columns seemed
The tree-trunks of their crowning woods. Some rose
All garlanded with yellow wreathèd light,
While others, draped with ivy, proudly towered
Like verdant obelisks, monuments to saints;
While here and there he saw, through mountain vistas,
Faint glimpses of arcades and mystic scenes,
Where purple shadows played and sunny smiles.
One little rill, so delicately tinged,
Like pale gold melted, spangled all the rocks
Where'er it fell, and pearl'd them o'er with beauty.
Sparkling and prattling, long he watched its course,
And poured his feelings in this little song—

> " Pure Rillet, how I long to be
>   In life both pure and glad like thee !—
>   So bright above, so bright below,
>   So eloquent thy babbling flow.
>   From rock to rock and day to day,
>   So fresh and merry in thy play—
>   Lone Rillet, sweet to me thy psalm,
>   Sung ever here in storm or calm.

> " All jubilant with flashing light,
>   In laughter leaping from thy height;
>   With shimmer'd spray of sparkling hues,
>   Far sprinkling down with dropping dews.

Would *I* could laugh and leap and sing,
And joy, as thou, around me fling !
Through all my course, oh, may I be
All beautiful in life like thee !

" What joy if *I* o'er sorrow's head,
Like thee, some hopeful gleams might shed ;
Or could I into sorrow's heart,
Like thee, some cheering light impart !
So frolicsome with buoyant rush,
So glad and gleeful in thy gush—
Oh, Rillet, how I long to be
In life both pure and bright like thee !"

Now swept a veil of trembling glory high
O'er rock and rillet, lake and waterfall ;
Till, softly floating on the halcyon air,
And bathing in the hues of Heaven, there came
A coronet of clouds enwreathing all.
Before this radiant and sun-burnished scene
He stood entranced, and thus his reverie ran—

" Grand gloried matter—rich, how rich thy spell !
Ye cold dead rocks, how bright with light ye seem
The crystal voices of your streams to me
Are echoing round the poetry of God !
But *late*, I could have laid me down and wept
Among the wrecks of fallen capitals,
Where the cakèd mouldiness of aged moss

Creeps dank o'er broken walls and human bones;
But *now* this blazonry of Nature's show,
This pomp of water, rock, and gorgeous sky,
Has lifted up the longings of my heart,
To mingle with the gladdening joy they shed,
And blend my being with the Power that folds
This great pavilion of the Universe.
Ye altar hills—pageants of mountain-power!
Lovely as mighty! beautiful as thrones
Of Nature—cheered and happy 'now,' my heart,
E'en like the quiet waters at your feet,
Is filled with the image of your loveliness,
And joys in Him who made you what you are!"

The "Astræa,"

GUARDSHIP AT FALMOUTH.

(ABOUT 1832.)

● ● ●

SOFT o'er the waters, where thou sittest in pride,
    The moonlight fell;
No murmur broke upon the halcyon heavens
    Save of silvery ripples,
That o'er the deep and quiet waters played,
Like feelings o'er the faces of the beautiful.

The harbour slept within its girdling hills,
    And all was hushed
Till thou, long tenant of its changeful waves,
Didst deeply thunder with thy cannon-voice
The curfew-hour and claim my thoughts.

Thy floating shadow fell upon the deep,
    Even as a tune upon the heart,
    With soft and quiet impress.
I then bethought me—musing. All around
Is shadowy and changeful as thine image—
    These ships, whose naked masts

Now rise like silver columns on the sea,
But harbour *here* awhile and then are gone !
   And aged men in years gone by,
Their brows besprinkled with the snows of time,
Have stood where now I stand and looked on thee ;
    But now, the grass is greening o'er them
    And they sleep forgotten.

Fond childhood, too, with all its budding hopes,
    So gay and happy-hearted,
Has paced this terrace, looking long on thee ;
But fresh'ning dews now sparkle on the sod
    That hides it from our eyes.

The strong young man, in life's bright lustihood,
    Counting on length of days,
Perchance beloved of one whose early grief
    In silent desolation told
How dear the memory of his trusting love—
    Yes, even he, so glad in hope,
While yet the glory of his youth was fresh,
Has walked thy decks and shared thy festal joys ;
    But now a blank is in his home,
And oft a quiet smile of starry light
    Is beaming where he sleeps ;
But *thou* art still the same, though youth and age,
The silver honours of the hoary head
    And bright locks of the beautiful,
Pass into dust alike and are forgotten !

Whether the morning-break come mellowing down,
Cresting thy wavelets with a golden light;
Or whether it open with a stormy scowl,
    Tumbling the waves about thee;
Whether the twilight of the Evening hour
      Fall calmly as the light of hope
      On childhood's happy dream;
Or night's deep darkness muffle round thy hull,
When only flickerings of thy cabin-lights
Tell where thou cradlest in the hollow surge,
      Battling with billow,—
      Yet in all unchanged,
Thou sitt'st enshrined within thy watery home,
      Like virtue in a good man's heart,
Or like some Phidian grace whose sculptured smile
      Plays on for ever;
While, o'er earth's transient pageants rolling,
      The surge of ages sweeps
And dashes its broken altars down!

Meleager's Lament at the Tomb of Heleodora.

* * *

LONE, o'er the quiet greening spot
    Where thou art sleeping,
I love to bend, though thou canst not
    Behold me weeping,
My flowing grief—poor fond relief—
    Bedews thy grave,
       Heleodora,
    Bedews thy grave,
And yet, though *here* thou must remain,
Since earth takes back her own again,
    Thou still art mine,
       Heleodora,
    Thou still art mine!

Alas! alas!—for where is now
    The loveliest flower
That ever smiled upon my path
    In life's best hour?—
It's spotless bloom is in the tomb,
    For Thou art there,
       Heleodora,
    For Thou art there!

Oh, earth! thou grave of all the dead,
 Nor less their mother,
Her softly to thy bosom fold,
 For not another
Of all that rest in thy cold breast
 Is mourned like thee,
  Heleodora,
Is mourned like thee.
Fond memories of thy morning bloom
To me still blossom o'er thy tomb,
 For thou art mine,
  Heleodora,
Thou *still* art mine!

Farewell.

TO A CITY ENDEARED BY MANY HAPPY REMINISCENCES.

* * *

BRIGHT City, now farewell!
Thou e'er to me didst wear a welcome smile
    When life's fond hopes were high;
In memory I have thought on thee awhile
    And mused on things gone by.
I *still* would linger, but it must not be—
The link is broken binding me to thee;
    Bright City, now, farewell!

    And I have said farewell
To many scenes and friends of other years.
    All now are past and gone—
Their vanishing deep-felt and felt with tears,
    My sorrow shared by none.
1 would recall them just as they have been,
But never more by me can they be seen—
    Forever now, "Farewell!"

On the Death of Prince Henry of Battenberg.

• • •

A PRINCE has fallen far away,
No pleasure-pilgrim, soft and gay,
  But chivalrous and brave;
A hero's gallant heart he bore
To battle on a foreign shore,
  Through swamps and perils grave.

No pageantries of royal life
Availed to keep him from the strife
  For England's cause and fame;
The blazonries of princely state,
The pomp of life so high and great,
  Were as an empty name.

No! not the fear of shot and shell
With coward-qualms his heart could quell
  Where dangers dread were nigh—
Not death that filled the poisoned air,
And made the swamp the soldier's lair,
  Whereon to fall and die.

The glory of our arms he sought,
All else awhile he deemed as nought,
  All princely pride laid down;
Nor would have shrunk by doughty deeds,
Even where the common soldier bleeds,
  To serve the British Crown.

But, as a soldier's death he found,
Condoling nations all around
  In England's sorrow share;
He went to champion England's right,
Her lofty dignity and might—
  For these, all foes to dare.

Alas! his dark disastrous fate
Has left a palace desolate,
  A widowed Queen and Wife;
His children, too—his sweet home-flowers,
His playmates in the royal bowers—
  How saddened now their life!

How loved his light that on them shone,
Which light is now for ever gone
  From them, from Wife, from Queen!
Of all his kindly care bereft,
Still, still this soothing thought is left—
  How good and kind he'd been!

     Lyrics of a Life.

And were no public tribute paid,
His memory now will never fade—
  Ne'er from the throne depart;
No eulogy in bronze or song
His name is needed to prolong—
  'Tis writ on England's heart.

Australia.

* * *

ALONE and vast—fit home for kings—
  Bright throned on southern seas,
A youthful nation round her springs
  And free as is the breeze.
Full many a city her sons have raised
  Where forests dense once were,
E'en turning the bush into stately streets,
  And to gardens, the bushman's lair.

Chorus—

> Then on—sound on—Australia,
>   Lift high your glorious glee—
> Lift, lift your patriot plaudits high,
>   Your songs of Liberty!

She has sons of the field, of the mine and the wave,
  A nation's pride and power;
Their sinews are strong and their hearts are brave,
  Of chivalry the flower.

With a hero's pluck and a hero's arm
  Her swarthy foes she met,
And young and strong her triumph-tree
  Of glorious Freedom set.

   Chorus—

      Then on—sound on—Australia,
        Lift high your glorious glee—
        Lift, lift your patriot plaudits high,
        Your songs of Liberty!

The Queen of all these southern Isles,
  She is rearing fast a race
To flourish ages yet to come
  And hold a foremost place—
She is rearing a race in a glorious land,
  An empire yet to be,
With daughters as fair and with sons as grand
  As any in history!

   Chorus—

      Then on—sound on—Australia,
        Lift high your glorious glee—
        Lift, lift your patriot plaudits high,
        Your songs of Liberty!

Old London.

• • •

THE London of a few gone years,
  Say sixty years ago,
How changed and grown it now appears!
  And will it always grow,
Great giant city of the earth,
  The greatest here below?

On what it was, when I look back,
  But sixty years ago,
What crowds of changes in the track
  Of years that swiftly flow!
Old scenes are gone and new come on
  In movements quick or slow.

No railway neared its swelling bounds,
  But sixty years ago;
No omnibus pursued its rounds
  In journeyings to and fro;
No uniformed police were seen
  On watch for robber-foe.

No penny-journal of all views,
  But sixty years ago,
Each morning told the daily news,
  Or when a storm would blow;
No letter for a penny then
  Through all the realm could go.

No gas illumed the streets at night,
  E'en sixty years ago—
Dim oil-lamps flickered with dull light,
  In broken zig-zag row;
Of telegraphs and telephones
  Nought then did science know.

What bridges spanned the tidal march,
  But sixty years ago,
No more uphold the crumbling arch
  Above the ebb and flow;
"Old London" now and "Westminster"[1]
  No gloomy shadows throw.

Down fell in fiery heaps th' Exchange,
  Since sixty years ago—
Down fell in lurid flames as strange
  The Senate-Houses low;
But prouder piles now take their place
  For business and for show.

---

[1] Bridges.

The prisons now, so grim and lone,
  But sixty years ago,
Were things "to come," for not a stone
  Lay in its base below;
Then Holloway and Pentonville
  Screened neither crime nor woe.

But some have fallen at Ruin's feet,
  Unmourned their overthrow;
The Compter, Fleet, and Whitecross Streets,
  Unsorrowed let them go;
What wrecks *have been*, and left no trace,
  Since sixty years ago!

The postman with his bell and bag,
  But sixty years ago,
Collected letters, though a rag
  Might in his garments show;
The town-crier shouted, "Stolen or strayed!"
  With lusty lungs, I trow.

Bronzed foreigners with dancing bears,
  Since sixty years ago,
With camels, serpents, monkeys, players,
  Through London Streets might go,
And gather coppers of the crowd
  That thronged to see the show.

Now, products from remotest Mains
  To London markets flow—
The cattle of a thousand plains
  In thousands thither go;
Yet these great markets were unknown
  But sixty years ago.

What, London, shall thy greatness be
  As on the ages roll?
Thy power gone out from sea to sea,
  Is felt from pole to pole;
Great growing magazine of earth—
  The world's inspiring soul!

Old England.

(SONG OF HER PATRIOTS.)

(SET TO MUSIC.)

• • •

EMPRESS of States around,
  Grand on the battle-plain,
Mother of heroes bold,
  Queen of the ocean-main;
Armies of England, Hail!
  Braver were never known;
Navies of England, Hail!
  Glory of England's throne!

Then beat the drum,
The trumpets blow,
And let encircling nations know
Old England fears no foe!

Soldiers, your Waterloo—
  Sailors, your Trafalgar—
Won for England fame
  Round the great world afar!

Champions of England's Queen,
　Wielding her battle-guns,
Bravely her foes confront,
　Ye are her champion sons !

　　Then beat the drum,
　　The trumpets blow,
　And let encircling nations know
　　Old England fears no foe !

Far as the waves can roll,
　England has conqueror been—
Proud of her dauntless Braves,
　Proud of her gracious Queen ;
Sing, then, the Nation's Song,
　Lift it in thunder grand—
England is Freedom's home,
　England, the patriot's land !

　　Then beat the drum,
　　The trumpets blow,
　And let encircling nations know
　　Old England fears no foe !

Stanzas,

Partly in Northern Dialect.

• • •

WHAT jocund chiel' o' naïve mirth,
Fra' t' greenest isle o' all the earth,
Now quits the bound of its water-girth?
           Kathleen Magee.

Who, ne'er fasht[1] a bit while to roam,
Now rides o'er crests o' the Channel foam
To glad the hearth of an English home?
           Kathleen Magee.

Who, when there, wi' gladsome chang,[2]
Chattit and laughed the heale[3] day lang,
And blithely chantit a bonnie sang?
           Kathleen Magee.

---

[1] "fasht"—from the French *fâcheux*.   [2] "chang"—noise.
[3] "heale"—whole.

Who jeybed[1] as clish-ma-clash[2] and blarney
The blazour'd[3] name o' Persiani,
And thowt her style owr[4] faussement garni?
       Kathleen Magee.

Who clumb[5] wi' cluits[6] that howk'd[7] the brant
O' Shepherd's Crag, and doon the slant
Sae doucely toppled[9] where storm-clouds haunt?
       Kathleen Magee.

Who there, enthroned on rigid bink,[10]
Old Skiddaw scanned from dizzy brink,
Then eyed the lake, then hied to drink?
       Kathleen Magee.

Who laughed on " Ulls's[11] dimpled feace,[12]
Like fansome[13] lass o' the pools o' Greece,
And thowt[14] the scene a bonnie pleace?
       Kathleen Magee.

Who, like a cliff-o'erhanging flower,
Looked dawnth[15] screes[16] by Lyulph's tower,
While resting in the swelting[17] hour?
       Kathleen Magee.

---

[1] " jeybed "—gibed.
[2] " clish-ma-clash "—foolish talk.
[3] " blazour'd "—praised.
[4] " owr "—over.
[5] " clumb "—climbed.
[6] " cluits "—feet.
[7] " howk'd "—scooped a foothold.
[8] " brant "—steep.
[9] " toppled "—fell.
[10] " bink "—a stone seat.
[11] " Ulls's "—Ullswater's.
[12] " feace "—face.
[13] " fansome "—kind, affectionate.
[14] " thowt "—thought.
[15] " dawnth "—down the.
[16] " screes "—precipices.
[17] " swelting "—hot.

Who neist[1] gang'd doon t' Airy Force
And scanned aboon his thunder-course,
And thowt his voice was awfu' hoarse?
      Kathleen Magee.

But, ah! who'll lave, when she is geane[2]
Fra English scenes sae gladsome green,
A lang cauld blank where she hae been?
      Kathleen Magee.

---

[1] " neist "—next.   [2] " geane "—gone.

The Mountain Pilgrim of Cumberland.

(*A TRUE STORY.*)

* * *

His mantle girt with leathern band,
With satchel in his feeble hand,
   He, yearly without change,
Though whitened locks streamed down his head,
And o'er his aged shoulders spread,
   Trod all the mountain range.

In every house on mountain side,
Or farmstead where its waters glide,
   The pilgrim found a home;
The children on his knees at night
Would twist and twine his locks of light,
   And list his "Lays of Rome."

One Autumn sad, though on his way,
And o'er the mountains seen to stray,
   He reached no friendly door.
The Winter's stormy months went round,
The pilgrim-almsman no one found;
   'Twas said, "He'll come no more."

When Spring returned with smiles and bloom,
Some maidens climbed where thunders boom,
    And sudden—halt and stand !
Up there they found the old man dead,
No cover on his whitened head,
    His crook still in his hand.

His rotted satchel near him lay;
The bulbs it held had burst with May
    And rooted in the ground—
Their flowers were blooming gay and fair,
As if no lifeless form lay there,
    Unhid by sacred mound.

Thus runs the course of human life—
While thousands wrestling in its strife
    Fall dead, 'mid dead to lie,
Yet thousands more bloom on like flowers,
And frolic through life's sunniest hours,
    Nor reck that they must die.

K

On a Skeleton.

(Dug up near Scarboro' in 1834; supposed to be between two and three thousand years old.)

• • •

WHO is this, disrupted from the earth,
  Revisiting its life and light?
    One from the days of old;
Back to primal dust, from whence his birth,
  Where he should sleep the grave's long night,
    Crumbling again to mould,
He hath refused to go, though dread and stern
The fiat—"Dust, to dust thou must return."

What!—no fading script to tell his name;—
  His state, his deeds, his joys, his groans,
    Shrouded in shadows dim?
These poor relics—shrunk to *these* his fame?—
  A *pin*, some *berries* and these *bones*,[1]
    All that remain of him?
Oh, state! oh, power! oh, pomp!—what are ye *all*
When Time spreads o'er us his oblivious pall?

---

[1] These and some pieces of skin were the only things found in the large oak sarcophagus.

What thoughts sublime may once have filled this
    dome![1]
  What love made glad this hollow breast,
    Or in these sockets shone!
But now, such thoughts, such love have here no
    home!
  Who knows if *here* they e'er *did* rest?
    Gone!—yes, *forever* gone!
So time will wreck us *all* . . . no token spare
To tell hereafter *who* or *what* we were!

---

[1] Byron's metaphor for the skull.

* * *

How, like the promise of the Spring,
Beneath the cold blast withering,
Hath many a noble spirit gone,
Whom families looked coldly on
Because, if void of earthly state,
They deem no noble spirit great!

The proud prerogative of kings
Is not contempt of meaner things—
No warranty we grant the great
To mock at men of meaner state;
Yet thus is humble genius crushed,
And all its song for ever hushed.

Ah! little think the high of birth,
The noblest lineage of the earth
Is that of mind and not of blood,
Though *this* were traced beyond the flood!
Yet families of pedigree
Oft spurn the mind's nobility.

Through all the range of things we know—
From suns that blaze to worms that glow,
From dews that gem the morning grass
To seas that roll their mighty mass—
The unambiguous traces spring
Of Godhead in their fashioning.

They character each marked degree
Of all the human family,
Which graduates through every lot
From palace-home to rustic cot;
One interweaving tie we scan
Links state to state and man to man.

Why scorn then, ye of noble grade,
The noble man whom nature made?—
On blazoned pinnacles of power,
Bright thrones of dust, ye strut your hour—
When that is done, adown ye fall!
He lives in fame's eternal hall.

Nor ye who boast ancestral race,
Deem occupation a disgrace,
Or 'scutcheoned pride or heraldry
More worth than toil-worn honesty;
But though the brow with sweat be dewed,
There is no shame in servitude.

Rudolph Parting from Hilda.

• • •

Thou genius of departed times,
    I speak to thee,
Unshine the dreams of other years
    So dear to me—
    Those dreams that tell
    What loving spell
Will link us after parting.

Yes—though the hand of fate should write,
    " Ye two must sever,
No more to meet in youth or age,
    Nor yet forever,"
    Still love's sweet flower
    In memory's bower
Will bloom . . . and bloom forever!

Deep trace thy furrows in the sky,
    Thou tyrant, "Age"—
Yes, write thy wrinkles in the sea
    And quell his rage;
    But let thy flight
    Ne'er fling its blight
On what we vowed together.

Depart, all other tokens past—
    Yes, ye may fly!
Away all other dreams to come—
    Yes, ye may die!
    For I have shrined
    Within my mind
Fond visions of my Hilda.

The silver gleams of many moons
    Have waned and brightened
Since first we saw each other's homes,
    With hearts so lightened;
    Yet fresh the flower
    Of that fond hour
We twined and wreathed together.

And now, though all earth's finest things
    Decay and wither,
And though the tide of ceaseless change
    Is rolling hither;
    Yet on and on
    Till life is gone
Our love can know no changing.

The Buried Miners.

* * *

DEEP, swinging down the awful depth,
    They went to toil below ;
For this they left the smiles of home—
    The sweetest smiles we know ;
They laboured long where all was night,
To bless our hearths with warmth and light.

Alas ! a sulphurous blast of power
    At midnight shook the ground !
The shaft was closed, and from below
    Was heard no voice—no sound !
Then hopeless seemed the Miners' doom—
And that dark Pit—their mighty Tomb.

But rough, though noble, comrades strove
    To reach them night and day ;
While, down beneath, the Miners knelt
    For all at home to pray.
At last—oh, joy !—hark ! hark !—they're found !
Their cheers are echoing underground !

What gladness thrills the dizzy brink
   As up the Miners come,
And rush and cling to wife and child—
   Those cherished loves of home !
With shouts that ring from earth to sky,
   Then many voices cry—
" Cheer, cheer the Rescuers, glorious men !
Hip, hip—Hurrah !—Again !—Again ! "

Still They Sleep.

• • •

BESIDE a hillock often stand
  A sister and a brother;
They grieve for those that sleep below,
  Their father and their mother.
"How long," they say, "how long they lie!"
Though many days have flitted by—
      Still they sleep.

The Morning rises, fresh and bright,
  Their graves give forth no sound;
They wake not with the waking world
  'Neath this, their hallowed mound;
The Spring returns with all its flowers,
And Summer, with its rainbow showers—
      Still they sleep.

And Autumn-leaves have rustled here
  Where these sad willows wave,
While chimes and shadows oft have swept
  O'er this sequestered grave;
But though upon it lies the snow,
Or Spring or Summer grasses grow—
      Still they sleep.

Well, there's a golden land on high,
  Where we shall never weep,
Nor bend o'er where in death they lie,
  Nor say—" Yet still they sleep."
Where we shall say—" No more to sever,
Dear father, mother, here forever—
    At last we meet."

The Octogenarian.

• • •

O'ER *this* frail withered frame hath swept
  The breath of many years;
The blight of age hath o'er me crept,
  The verge of death appears;
Nor beam of Morn or Evening now
Can warm, *as once,* my chilly brow,
  Or freshen life's dull fires;
Nay—e'en to think of joys "that were"
Embitters more an old man's care,
  And no *new* hope inspires.

Old Time hath seen the wreck of all
  That ever smiled on me—
Myself ere long a wreck to fall,
  Far borne on life's dark sea.
Well—soothing thought, and yet how dread,
That I so soon must lay my head
  Down in its darksome cave!—
Yet, though all ties on earth are flown,
Christ sends me, from that State unknown,
  A welcome through the grave.

The Scarlet Lady.

(*A VISION.*)

• • •

SERENE from the twilight of times long departed,
  Illuming the gloom of unchronicled years,
The light of her youth on my visioning darted,
  As soft as the fall of the light of the spheres.

Around her the echoes of Shiloh were stealing,
  While Pagans unnumbered abandoned their shrines,
As throngs from all climes in her temples were
      kneeling,
  Their worship untrammelled by symbols or signs.

The homesteads of want and the mansions of power,
  The dungeons of darkness, the hidings of grief,
She sought out to bless, as a spirit whose dower
  Was joy for the joyless—for sorrow, relief.

She passed from my *dream*, but lo! crowding in
      numbers,
  Generations sped down to th' Eternity gone!
The sound of their rushing broke deep on my
      slumbers,
  As phantom-winged ages flew hurriedly on!

Again on my vision she came, but in seeming
  So changed that she wore scarce a trait of her
      youth ;
She looked as the *sorceress* of souls in my dreaming—
  The wanton of Rome teaching error for truth.

The power of her spells o'er the people extended—
  They bowed to her symbols and worshipped her
      signs ;
Her crosses and crosiers and altars were blended
  With dungeons and tortures, with faggots and
      shrines.

Thick swarmed through the nations her agents and
      orders,
  Her monks and confessionals, legates and pyres—
Her councils and conclaves, her abbots and warders,
  Her nuns and her priests, her pilgrims and friars.

I heard from the Vatican sounds of her cursing,
  When, lo ! a great kingdom groaned under her ban ;
In the churches no prayers—for the dying, no
      nursing,
  And praises to God through their aisles never ran.

Around lay the dead, whom she 'reft of sepulture—
  Dogs snarled as they crunched o'er their unsepulchred
      bones ;
With fetid corruption she glutted the vulture,
  Nor suffered the honours of grief-telling stones.

I saw her Tribunal—the nations affrighted,
  But whispered its name on the hush of their
      breath ;
There, gloating on tortures, she wantoned delighted,
  Enacting her horrible revels of death !

Time passed—when again, in the close of my
      dreaming,
  I saw her once more in the visions of night,
But changed—oh, how changed!—in her work and her
      seeming—
  For darkness, she *now* was all radiant with light.

I saw her in cottage, in palace, and prison,
  A merciful Church dropping gifts from her hand ;
From the errors of ages she seemed to have risen—
  A saintlier Vision, more blessed to the land.

The Contrast.

(*A DIALOGUE.*)

LÆTITIA, *the joyful one.*   TRISTITIA, *the sad one.*

* * *

LÆTITIA—Freshly the *Sun* shall yield his light
Till judgment toll;
The starry heraldry of night
Till then shall roll.

TRISTITIA—Yes, *they* shall sparkle to the unborn,
As ages pass,
While *I* shall sleep, nor wake at morn,
Beneath the grass.

LÆTITIA—The *Earth* looks young and fresh and green,
As in its prime;
'Tis beautiful—no wrinkle seen
Deep worn by Time.

TRISTITIA—Oh, say not so! in its first birth
It had no dead;
Now mark its heaps, and one, oh Earth!
Must be *my* bed.

LÆTITIA—The *Sea* majestically sweeps
  To every shore;
Travelling in power, its awful depths
  Heave evermore.

TRISTITIA—Ages it rolled ere I had breath,
  And ages on
Will roll, and whelm the loved in death,
  When I am gone.

LÆTITIA—All things are fresh, and all seem new—
  The breeze, the shower,
The blue of heaven, the morning dew,
  The twilight hour.

TRISTITIA—All fresh and new? Alas! each day
  Tells how they fly—
How childhood, youth and life's sweet May
  Pass swiftly by.

LÆTITIA—True—leaves and graves and death and birth
  All tell this truth,
Though Sea and Sun and Stars and Earth
  Have endless youth.

L

The Windmill.

● ● ●

Oft, how oft, we used to sit
  By this old mill in days gone by,
And breathe our vows, as round and round
  The circling wheel would seem to fly.
How like the wheel of life, I thought—
  Now down in gloom, now up in play;
A voice oft seemed amidst its sails,
  And this is what it seemed to say:—

" To Heaven's winds *I'm* always true,
  Ever rolling, rolling ever;
Will *you* and *he* be always true,
  Faithful ever, faithless never?"
Since then long years have passed away—
  Long years he's vanished from my sight;
Not true to *me*, as is this *wheel*
  To *winds of Heaven* by day and night.

The Windmill.

As thus she mused—lo ! lo ! he comes !
  Escaped the isles of barbarous men,
Where he had long ago been wrecked,
  And thought to see her ne'er again.
He clasped her fondly, fondly said—
  "I come to thee, the ocean o'er;
For, long as life's worn wheel shall turn,
  My heart is thine—true evermore !"

The Dear Old Fire.

• • •

How dear the old Home-Fire!
In long-lapsed nights of years gone by,
When wintry winds were whistling high,
We snugly listened to their sound,
And cosily all gathered round
 The bright, the Dear Old Fire!
While, on her knees, as roared the gales,
Our mother told us good old tales
 Beside the Dear Old Fire!

 I love the Dear Old Fire!
Where at the romp, the kiss, the glee,
The old folks laughed so merrily—
I love its smiling cheery glow,
A truer friend we ne'er shall know
 Than that—the Dear Old Fire!
One thing I hope, whate'er betide,
Still oft to come and sit beside
 The ever Dear Old Fire!

God bless the Dear Old Fire!
Sweet spell to bind us all to home,
To cheer us as through life we roam,
With all our future still to blend
Life's fondest mem'ries to the end—
  The loved, the Dear Old Fire!
Though gone the old folks, long mourned with
    tears,
In loving hearts will shine for years
  The dear—the Dear Old Fire!

He thinks He hears their Echoes.

• • •

Old and lone, he has lost his joys,
  As age has come creeping on,
But their echoes he thinks he hears,
  Though all his old joys are gone.
Though himself but an ended song,
  He still, as of old, would sing,
But his voice, now so broken and weak,
  Has lost all its good old ring.

Of the Angel that had blessed his youth,
  Of friends of his morning years,
Nought is left but a shadowy dream,
  His memories and his tears!
Still " he thinks that he hears the echoes "
  Of voices forever flown,
That have died down the stream of Time,
  And left him so old and lone.

Through the windows of all his Past
  He peers with a wistful gaze,
Though the faces are gone forever
  That smiled on his early days.
Could the Future but open wide
  Its windows so dusky and dim,
They would show the old man where now
  Those faces are watching for him.

She Fell like a Flower.

" Elle tomba comme une Fleur.
Qui n'a vu qu'une Aurore."
Tragédie d'Esther.—RACINE.

(*A Very Early Poem.*)

* * *

BESIDE a lake, embowered in trees,
  An ancient mansion rose—
There towering oaks defied the breeze,
  There blushed the vernal rose.
In groves of fragrance fountains played,
And arbours woo'd with friendly shade,
  As harps Æolian sighed;
Birds spread their plumes of velvet gold,
And waterfalls in music rolled
  Their rainbow-coloured tide.

Twas there that Gladys, radiant child,
  First saw the light of day—
There first she lisped in accents mild
  And 'guiled the hours away.
Light as the hart she tripped at morn—
Now played—the fairy of the lawn—

Now wandered 'midst the flowers;
And often, too, to rest resigned,
She lay on mossy seat reclined,
  In shade of quiet bowers.

'Twas not her form, that breathing spell,
  That bade home's love awake;
'Twas not her luty voice that fell
  Like moonlight on a lake;
'Twas not her laughing eye that gleamed,
Nor yet her golden locks that streamed
  Luxuriantly down,—
'Twas artless innocency flung
The floating charm that round her hung,
  Like soft-hued aureole-crown.

I looked again—but saw a blank
  Among earth's fondest daughters,
Yes—she was gone! Too soon she sank
  Down death's cold darkling waters.
Sad o'er her parents swept the token
Of blighted hope and spirits broken,
  Of ties 'tis hard to sever.
Their weeping told 'twas hard to part
Those interlinkings of the heart
  That snapped—are snapped forever!

Her favourite bower, now rude and lone,
  With leaves is scattered o'er—
Its beauteous visitant is flown,
  To visit it no more.

The lake, across whose smiling wave
Her life's first melodies she gave,
  Looks blank, for she—is where?
The bright cascade, sad sounds its fall,
And vacant seems the silent hall—
  She is not—is not there!

How like the bloom of flowering tree
  This guileless beauty fell!
How like the cloud that skims the sea
  Swept far her funeral knell!
Yet though the world, when all was o'er,
Went on its ways just as before,
  And scarce a thought did deign,
Long o'er her ashes many wept,
As calm in death her spirit slept,
  Which yet will wake again.

Angel, Child, and Flower.

(*A TRILOGUE.*)

Xmas.

• • •

ANGEL—Oh, hail ! thou little child of earth,
The story of thy Saviour's birth !
Long ages ere He came to thee,
He made the angel-hosts and me ;
Then, leaving Heaven, this earth he trod,
To make a child, a child of God.

CHILD—And are there children in the skies
That chant in angel-melodies ?
Did Jesus at this season come
To take them to His glorious home ?
Shall *I*, like thee, be made divine,
And up in Heaven in beauty shine ?

FLOWER—And are there flowers that bloom abovo,
Sweet on the Saviour's breast of love ?
And on His sceptre, crown, and throne,
And seraphs' harps of brightest tone ?
Then take me there to share with thee
Their bloomings through Eternity.

ANGEL—Yes, there are children in the skies
 That chant their angel-melodies!
 Yes, there are flowers that bloom above,
 Sweet on the Saviour's breast of love;
 And *all* the flowers and children there
 Are beautiful "beyond compare."

CHILD—Oh, will it not be sweet to me,
 With loveliest children there to be!
 To plash in fountains, soar on wings,
 And drink from Life's eternal springs;
 To walk with Jesus, bright and free—
 Oh, will it not be sweet to me!

FLOWER—Though brows of beauty I adorn
 With tints as fresh as smiles of morn;
 Though altars brighten with my bloom,
 And mourners wreathe me round the tomb;
 For flowers to deck the things of Heaven,
 What glory must to them be given!

ANGEL—One God for all—the child, the flower—
 For angels in their spheres of power;
 One Saviour came, divinely mild,
 To call to Heaven each little child;
 One Maker makes all bloom to blow,
 Of flowers above and flowers below.

The Flower=Girl.

(AT A CHARITY FANCY-FAIR.)

• • •

Roses I sell, of roses I sing—
Who'll come and buy the roses I bring?

See! here are some the sun has kissed
And made to blush with glowing hue,
Their cheeks still beaming with his smiles,
And freshened with the morning dew.
Much more than gems the rose's bloom
Doth grace the radiant bride's adorning,
More brightly deck her gallant knight
When robing for their bridal morning.

Roses I sell, of roses I sing—
Who'll come and buy the roses I bring?

Far back, in the great long ago,
A martyr-maiden braved the fire,
And from her ashes all the flames
Streamed up in roses from her pyre!

Then nightingales (old bards have sung)
  'Mid roses far more sweetly trilled,
And, with their loveliest evening hymns,
  More gushingly the gardens filled.

    Roses I sell, of roses I sing—
    Who'll come and buy the roses I bring?

For garlands or for festal halls,
  For wreaths on where tomb-grasses grow—
See! here are roses bright, and lilies—
  Lilies pure as dazzling snow;
For shrine or altar, grave or bridal
  (And each the loving heart uncloses),
Oh, buy of me a bunch of flowers—
  A pretty votive gift of roses!

    Roses I sell, of roses I sing—
    Who'll come and buy the roses I bring?

The Stranded Ship.

(Narrative in Verse of a Real Fact.)

(SET TO MUSIC.)

• • •

THE sun was bright, the gale was strong,
The gilded waves were rolled along,
  And shook the sounding shore;
A ship drew near with plunging bound—
A moment more, she heaved aground
  And sideways canted o'er.
Ebb'd far the tide for weary hours,
Back to re-flow with stormier powers
  Where helpless she was driven;
The tars strained hard their ship to heel,
But one fell pinned beneath the keel—
  Oh, help!—no help but Heaven!

Now, rolling on with booming swell,
The tide drew near—his wife as well;
  Her wailings thrilled the skies.
Streamed on the blast her flowing hair.
Shrieked down the gale her frantic prayer—
  "Oh, save!—oh, save!" she cries.

"One kiss, dear wife—once more!" he said,
"And wrap thy mantle round my head;
  I would not see the tide,
So soon to take my mortal breath
And whelm me in the waves of death—
  Good-bye, dear wife, good-bye!"

The tide rolled on, the ship was heaved,
And late, *too* late, his limbs relieved—
  His quick-quenched life had fled!
His form on ebbing storm-waves cast,
Far on the sands was left at last,
  So desolately dead!
She knelt beside him, kissed his brow,
Wept streaming tears, and, resting now
  Her cheek upon his breast,
"Thy heart beats not—'tis still!" she cried;
"Yet—yet *again* I'll be thy bride,
  When both shall be at rest."

The Life-Boat Crew.

(SET TO MUSIC.)

• • •

Oh, fearful night!—th' Eternal Sea—
How loud and wild its revelry!
  Its billows—how they roll and leap!
Th' Eternal Heaven over all
Is muffled in its blackest pall
  And mingled with the thundering deep!

    Alas! this night for those at sea—
    How fearful must their peril be!

But lo!—afar a fitful glare—
Lo! rockets rush and upward flare;
  Some ship is hurled upon a shoal!
Her sails are shreds, her boats are gone,
And in her rigging men hold on,
  While towering surges o'er them roll.

                         M

Loud sounds the echoing signal-gun ;
Quick to the shore the people run—
　The Life-boat Crew are off—away !
Now high on storm-lashed billows tossed,
Now low in deep abysses lost,
　In blinding squalls and snow and spray

From whistling cordage quick unlashed
The men are saved, all tempest dashed—
　Proud honour to the Life-boat Crew !
They battle back through howling strife
With all their precious freight of life ;
　"Bravo the gallant Life-boat Crew ! "
"Bravo ! " and "benedictions " loud
Shout up to Heaven the excited crowd.

Yesterday.

• • •

THE starry heraldry of night,
Planets [1] from constellations bright,
    Have passed away—
So hope that now my future decks
May vanish soon with all the wrecks
    Of yesterday!

The sweetest joys of life to me,
That cheered my path so merrily,
    Soon passed away—
And all to which my heart now clings,
Ere long, will be with bygone things
    Of yesterday!

Where now my childhood's happy days?
My youth's fond dreams—hope's onward gaze?
    All passed away—
Where now the idols of my heart,
From which it darkened life to part?
    With yesterday!

---

[1] Disappearance of stars—*See* Tycho Brahe, 1572; Montanire, 1670, &c.

What once I prized as home's sweet bliss—
The household love, a mother's kiss—
    Soon passed away;
And cheering dreams of coming years
Are mingled now with wasted tears
    Of yesterday!

'Tis well to seize the golden hours,
Ere yet they all, like faded flowers,
    Have passed away—
Life's "mission-time" each moment glides,
Till we sweep down th' eternal tides
    Of yesterday!

What happiness we lose to-day,
What thousand hopes are cast away,
    Because, O sorrow!
We blindly spurn the passing now,
For chiefest things no time allow,
    But the unknown to-morrow!

The Poor Old Horse.

• • •

Who, in the rush of his thunder-tread,
With a lordly toss of his haughty head,
Away, away with the hunters sped?—
    The poor old Horse.

Who, with impetuous mettle bold,
Bounded on o'er the trackless wold,
Or champed the bit, or rampant rolled?—
    The poor old Horse.

Who wantoned once in glorious might,
In proud curvets and trappings bright,
With spreading chest and eye of light?—
    The poor old Horse.

Who fearless rushed with flying mane
Triumphant o'er the battle-plain,
But fell not with the happier slain?—
    The poor old Horse.

Who to the far-off echoing neigh
Bounded off in his wild young play,
But *now* is lame and lank and grey?—
　　The poor old Horse.

Who, in his young and better days,
Pranced gleaming on in Glory's blaze,
But *now* drags hard up heavy ways?—
　　The poor old Horse.

Who, decked with dark and waving plume,
Once bore e'en princes to their tomb,
But *now* must bide a heartless doom?—
　　The poor old Horse.

Who oft, with gorgeous trappings gay,
Hath swelled the pomp of a bridal day,
But, spavined and galled, now limps away?—
　　The poor old Horse.

Who, straining, draws the oppressive load,
And unresisting bears the goad,
And then is driven to graze the *road?*—
　　The poor old Horse.

Who in the time of his glowing blood
E'er served his master all he could,
But *now* is weak for lack of food?
　　The poor old Horse.

Who tells, by gaunt and jaded bones,
The drudging slave of human drones,
How man is callous as the stones?—
    The poor old Horse.

Who tells what man himself may be
When age comes on or friends may flee,
Though none so buxom now as he?—
    The poor old Horse.

The War-Horse.

FRANCE—AN ALLEGORY.

(Translated from the French.)

• • •

BEAUTEOUS land of gallant daring,
  In the prime of Messidor—
France, how like a tameless charger,
  Free to range the desert o'er !
Never curbed by bit or bridle,
  Sporting wild 'midst forest trees ;
Never touched by hand of mortal,
  Free as is the desert breeze.
Darting round her fiery glances,
  High her nostril-steamings curl'd ;
Wild she bounded, mad and mighty,
  And her neighings shook the world !
Then He[1] marked her—Prince of Warriors
  Pawing in her native plain ;
Fierce was she, but He yet fiercer,
  And did grasp her streaming mane,

---

[1] Napoleon.

Vaulting on the maddened creature,
  Forth to war they sped away;
For they loved the voice of trumpets,
  And the battle-charger's neigh.
Rushing on through cannon-thunders,
  Whizzing ball, aud clashing shield;
On and on he madly drove her—
  All the world her battle-field.
Morning broke—she had not slumbered;
  Evening fell—to her unblest;
Noontide blazed—she still was raging;
  Night came on—she found no rest.
Plunging wild o'er scattered corpses,
  Trampling fiercely 'mid the dead—
Many a year she trode the nations,
  Many a year the nations bled!
Spent at last her lusty mettle,
  Down she fell o'er heaps of slain—
Cravèd rest of her restless rider,
  But He lashed her up again.
Foaming on, she faltered, beaten—
  Panting, gasping hard for breath;
Down she rolled in reeking slaughter,
  Wallowing on the field of death.
Then her Rider—mighty warrior!—
  Mightiest of the sons of men!
Warded by the ocean [1] waters,
  Ne'er could scourge the earth again.

---

[1] South Atlantic.

Plaint of the Convicts' Child.

(Rhythm and Air—"The Peace of the Valley.")

• • •

MANY years ago the daughter of two convicts, who were under sentence of transportation for life, went to the sea-shore to take a last view of the vessel which was taking them away from her forever.

That vessel, as it sank and rose in the wide and troubled waters, was perhaps no inapt emblem of her own coming lot on the sea of her future life. It was reported in a newspaper that she stood a long time watching and weeping till the vessel was out of sight.

The circumstance occasioned the following :—

THE hopes of my childhood are fled,
  The peace of Life's once happy hours ;
My parents are both doomed to tread
  No more 'mong our sweet cottage flowers.
And *now* the lone child of their love
  Must pine till she sleep with the dead ;
No more can she wander with them in the grove—
  The hopes of my childhood are fled.
     The hopes, &c.

Their ship o'er the wild billow strays,
  The heavens look gloomy and stern ;
And sad—ah, how sad !—'tis to gaze
  At those who can never return.
Between us will roll the wide main ;
  In grief must they pillow their head ;
I sigh for my parents, but ah ! 'tis in vain—
  The hopes of my childhood are fled.
          The hopes, &c.

The Midnight Storm.

* * *

THE Spirit of Night his black banner unfurls,
  The worlds of all heavens in his darkness he
    shrouds,
Proud navies suspends upon "billowy curls,"
  And wheels his dread throne on tempestuous
    clouds.

Hark! hark!—'twas the voice of the King of the
      Storm!
  The pillars of nature seemed rocked by the crash!
See! see!—oh! a shadowy, cloud-muffled form,
  Illumed by the glare of a quick-glancing flash!

Omnipotent heavens!—the Universe shook
  As fearful in thunders he muttered his ire!
Oh, horrors eternal!—how dread 'tis to look—
  The firmament blazes with flickering fire!

The cold wretch unhoused, from her lair of the
      ground
  Now starts up aghast 'mid the red-forkèd gleams—
A wild look she throws on the horrors around,
  And pours mid the howls of the tempest her
    screams.

See yonder scared maidens, half-clad as they rose,
  Rush forth from their homes o'er the flash-lighted
      sod,
Their pathway wild gleaming with fire as it glows
  In their chambers just lit by the dread bolt of God.

Unsepulchred burst from the grave of the past
  The ghosts of life's sins as if gifted with breath,
And wicked men quail at the horrible blast
  That rushes wild maddening and laden with death.

Sublime o'er the world the Almighty One rides—
  The hollow of heaven He fills with His form ;
Yet calm on the wing of the hurricane strides,
  Pavilioned in whirlwinds and girded with storm.

From His chariot of darkness weird thunderings fly,
  Loud rattling through Nature in world-shaking
      peals ;
O'er the skirts of the tempest that blacken the sky
  Gleam lurid the lightnings that flash from its
      wheels.

Yet rejoice, for the far-reaching Storm is His slave,
  As majestic through heaven its great echoings
      boom—
Rejoice as when morning mists walk from the wave,
  Or evening airs winnow the balm of the bloom.

Johnnie and Jeannie,

Workhouse Children.

(*A CHRISTMAS DIALOGUE.*)

• • •

JOHNNIE—The time for joy is coming, Jeannie,
    That used to make me glad,
But now our lot is darkened,
    And Christmas makes me sad.

JEANNIE—Before our father died, Johnnie,
    And mother's days were done,
A happy time was Christmas—
    What joy, what play, what fun !

JOHNNIE—They made the logs blaze high, Jeannie,
    Shut out the wind and snow,
And round the fire we gathered,
    To catch the rosy glow.

JEANNIE—And father taught us games, Johnnie,
    And nursed us on his knees,
    And told us merry tales,
    While hard the night did freeze.

JOHNNIE—And mother gave us toys, Jeannie,
    And clasped us to her breast,
    And sang us holy carols,
    Of Him, the new-born Guest.

JEANNIE—That merry time is gone, Johnnie,
    Our home—the workhouse *now;*
    No seat on father's knee, *here,*
    No kiss on mother's brow.

JOHNNIE—If only they could see us, Jeannie,
    Within these dreary walls,
    Their tears would fall in Heaven,
    Where tear-drop never falls.

JEANNIE—I cannot bear their loss, Johnnie,
    And Christmas makes me sad,
    Although when they were with us,
    It always made me glad.

JOHNNIE—Oh, do not fret so much, Jeannie!
    For they were God's own flowers—
    He plucked them when he pleased,
    To grow in Heavenly bowers.

JEANNIE—Will no one come to see us, Johnnie,
　　　　With Christmas smiles and cheer?
　　　　Will all the world forsake us
　　　　Because our home is *here?*

JOHNNIE—Oh, let us kneel and pray, Jeannie,
　　　　And let our weeping end,
　　　　For though we feel forsaken,
　　　　Yet God will be our friend.

A Father's Farewell.

(On the occasion of his Daughter's Marriage.)

● ● ●

THY bridal is a joy, Minnie,
  It also is a sorrow—
We smile with thee to-day,
  To weep thee gone to-morrow.

A daughter dear to me, Minnie,
  Through all thy life's young day—
A blank thou leav'st to me,
  And I am growing grey.

Thy brothers feel thy going, Minnie,
  Thy sisters shed their tears;
'Tis hard to say " Good-bye,"
  So loved through bygone years.

We yield thee up to one, Minnie,
  Proved worthy of thy heart,
To brighten all thy years
  Till comes the hour to part.

N

We know he'll guard thee well, Minnie
  And strive thy life to cheer—
Thou art his Heaven on earth,
  And he to thee most dear.

Yet sorrow comes to all, Minnie,
  And grief, and tears, and pain;
If such be thine and his,
  May joy soon come again.

With all thy wrecks of hope, Minnie,
  Thy tears will sadden me;
With every hope fulfilled,
  Thy joy will gladden me.

Be choicest blessings thine, Minnie,
  Of basket and of store—
Be sunny pleasure thine
  Till mortal things are o'er!

On Life's wide ocean now, Minnie,
  Thy sail begins to-day;
With thee our hopes will go,
  For thee our hearts will pray.

May God through life, to both, Minnie,
  Grant brighest cheery weather,
That you for many years
  May sail in love together!

There's "one" not here to-day, Minnie,
  Who reared thee at her side;
Thy mother—how would she
  Have blessed thee as a bride!

Her spirit looking down, Minnie,
  Will hover o'er thy life,
Rejoicing thou art now
  A fond and happy wife.

The Old Oak.

• • •

THOUGH now leafless and blighted,
  How majestic its prime,
When defying the tempests,
  When wrestling with Time !
Little children beneath it
  Used to sing and to play,
As their fathers before them,
  As *their* children to-day.
Then let its old honours long memoried be,
For loved all around was the Grand Old Tree !

Through its hundreds of summers
  Sat Old Age in its shade—
There the gay-hearted frolicked,
  There the Youth met his Maid ;
But the pride of the glory
  Of the Old Oak is dead,
With the children that loved it,
  In the years that are fled.
Still, still let its honours long memoried be,
For loved all around was the Grand Old Tree !

Demos; or, The New Electorate.

• • •

UP with shrines to mighty Demos,
 "Vulgus" of the Roman tongue—
Gather round and burn your incense,
 Shout his praise with brazen lung!
Fawn or flatter, fire or cool him,
Yet beware how you befool him!

Demos—power of sons of labour,
 Grim electorate of the law—
Scares his terror-struck creators,
 Hides iconoclastic claw;
Newest chief of State-directors,
Juggernaut of *old* electors.

Seek ye glory in the Commons?
 Fondly ask his vote for you;
Gild your baits and "promise wildly'—
 Cows and acres—these will do!
Fail in these—you court disaster,
For . . . he's now your lord and master.

Gather round the shrine of Demos—
　Well we know why 'tis you greet it;
When the eagles seek the carcase,
　Is it not that they may eat it?
New electors, hold them to it—
What they *promise*—or else rue it.

When they tell you lands of nobles,
　Settlements of thousand years,
All the mansions, all the castles,
　All the riches of all peers,
But await your grand division—
Growl your scorn and grin derision!

When they say the Church must go—
　Heritage from times of old,
Tithes, endowments, houses, glebe,
　All for *you* to *share* when sold—
Sacrilegious scrimmage! No!
Blood for blood *ere that* would flow!

High cathedrals, old and grand,
　Venerable churches where,
Noblest temples of the land,
　All our fathers knelt in prayer—
Would they *these* from God's use sever?
Rise and thunder—"Never, never!"

Barns and pig-sties would they build
  With our churches' holy walls,
And for romp, and dance, and song,
  Turn cathedrals into halls?
Bribe they thus, the wily snakes—
Let them heed when Demos wakes!

Guard the turf where sleep your fathers,
  Mothers, brothers, dear ones, all—
Never let them cart a cartful
  Of the church or church-yard wall.
No! Cry, "No!—no havoc *there!*
Those are *ours*—don't touch—don't dare!

Not your altars, not your fires,
  While you breathe above the sod,
Not the green graves of your sires,
  Not the churches of our God,
Let them barter for a seat,
Though to be M.P. is sweet.

Let your Church in faith and form
  Down to generations go;
Let your children, ages onward,
  In her life and doctrine grow—
But o'er her wrecks let traitors quail
St Stephen's slippery heights to scale.

The Present Distress.

"This is a day of trouble."—EZEKIEL.

*(Written in a time of great distress, fifty-four
years ago—i.e., up to the date of this Book—and
copied into a newspaper in St Lucia, one of the
West India Islands.)*

• • •

I SAW, where I never had seen it before,
The passing of Grandeur by Poverty's door;
O'er the hearthstone within, where the desolate
    wept,
A gleam of the brilliant pageant had swept.
The poor turned his eye on the pomp of the great,
But soon let it fall on his own wretched state;
He looked on his child, as it wept on his knee—
Why rang not its voice with a child's happy glee?
He looked on his wife, as she pined by his side—
Want—withered and wasted, her beauty had died.
Then round on his desolate home did he gaze,—
In that home was no food, on his hearth was no
    blaze;
With a gloom on his hopes that once brighter
    had shone,
He turned to the pageant—the pageant had gone.

"Not" (such were his words)—"not the dark-
  plumèd hearse,
Had it gone by my door, could have saddened
  me worse;
'Twere better to see it go on with the dead,
Than witness these loved ones thus pining for bread.
This pompous parade—and yet wherefore repine?
Should *I* parade less if such grandeur were mine?
Go, great one, be happy!—I would not on thee
Such sorrow should fall as has fallen on me."

But *why* look alone on this desolate few?
As the pageant proceeded such instances grew;
In each street was the voice of the famine-struck
    cry,
Which the great one much felt as he slowly
    passed by.

In the glorious *Heaven* I look on the *Sun*—
All freshly he glows as if just but begun;
On the *Ocean* below, and the rush of his tide
To the world's thousand ports rolls the swell
    of his pride;
On the green blooming *Earth*, and, lo! fresh from
    her hills,
Come sparkling in beauty her nutrient rills.
All fertile the valley, exhaustless the mine,
Unfailing the flock, nor unfruitful the vine,
As far round the world as the all-circling air—
These publish to man—"There's enough and to
    spare."

Then why is there want when abundance we find ?—
If God is so bounteous, who is unkind ?
Is it sleights in finance, or sharp tricksters in
    stocks ?
Is it policies, politics, gluts in the docks ?
Is it gatherers of riches that pile up their store,
Though having abundance yet piling up more ?
Is it these, the big builders of fortune so great,
That have crowded with poor the proud track
    of their state?
But seek, oh, ye statesmen ! if ye have the power,
To bless a crushed class in the straits of this hour !
In the depths of just counsels devise a just plan
For softening his hardships to poor honest man.
Your channels of commerce make free to the
    world—
Be its flag to the eyes of all nations unfurled ;
That each may serve each by the right of
    exchange,
As far as our race hath extended its range.
Who would *then* need to echo the voice of his
    wail
To the song of the bird that enlivens the gale,
Or look up to Heaven, with sorrow-dimmed sight,
When the gleaming sun glows in the noon of
    his might?
Through the range of all life in earth's mighty
    span,
No creature that breathes should be happier
    than Man.

The Anarchists.

• • •

GANG of murderers—ruthless, savage,
  Banded blood and brains to shed,
Vain of being Anarch-demons,
  Weirdly glorying o'er your dead—
Tell us *why* you plot and plan,
Plot to kill your fellow-man?
Bootless, senseless is your scheme—
Senseless as an idiot's dream.

Tell us *why* o'er death ye feast,
  Revelling in assassination,
Lower sunk than wildest beast—
  Gang, at war with every nation?
Treacherous, pitiless is your game,
Yet we know not what your aim;
O'er all such God's vengeance rides—
On all such man's curse abides.

Like as in the Apocalypse,
  Death, the Pale Horse, rode in blood,
They would trample, crush and slay
  All our great men—all our good.

Victims slain they ne'er deplore—
Fierce as Erymanthean boar,
Or Cleonian lion dread,
Gloating o'er the murdered dead.

Statesmen, wealth, and thrones, their spite—
　These, with *these* their barbarous war;
Rebels 'gainst both man and right,
　Rebels 'gainst both God and law.
Retribution—worthy fate—
Be their doom by laws they hate!
Ripe are they for demons' mirth—
Fit for scourging through the earth!

Festal hours they choose for blood,
　Heed they neither old nor young;
Full though theatre, senate, church,
　There their deadly bombs are flung.
'Mid the havoc of the crash,
'Mid the groans, the shrieks, the smash,
They themselves seek thence to fly,
In their secret haunts to lie.

Down to generations far,
　Loathed their memory—loathed their dust;
Enemies of mankind they are—
　Massacre their fiendish lust;
Outlawed, hunted, let them be—
"Driven from men" from sea to sea;
Then the earth once more shall rest
Free from this inhuman pest.

Anarchy !—that ghastly birth,
　Proud all Governments to scare—
Must be swept from off the earth,
　Laws and States must slay the slayer.
Rise then Italy, France, and Spain—
Rise in wrath—*avenge your slain !*
Seize the murderers at their work,
Spare them not where'er they lurk !

Theirs the logic armed with bombs,
　Rhetoric of the knife and dagger ;
Monsters, though in human form—
　Fiendish their ferocious swagger.
When their weapon plunges deep,
Making gallant nations weep,
When their red flag streams unfurled,
They defy the indignant world.

Ibester, the Lunatic.[1]

• • •

"Oh, take—oh, take me, Sir!" she calls;
"I want to leave these dreary walls[2] —
I long again to Heaven to climb,
Where once I lived in happier time.
My children all—the beauteous seven,
Sweet things of love—were born in Heaven.

"See!—*there* all streaming down the sky
Those amber clouds o'er mountains high—
Through *them* from Heaven to earth I rode,
My chariot bright with diamonds glowed;
Oh, were I back among the shrines
Where angels meet and sip their wines!

"*Then, there,* my little dear ones play;
Do take me up,—away—away!
In garden bowers they romp and roam,
That stately palace is their home;
With them the angels dip their feet
And plash in fountains where they meet."

---

[1] The above verses record her actual delusions.
[2] Union Workhouse.

Poor Hester ! Ne'er was lovelier bride,
But soon, too soon, her husband died !
No link was left—no child—no token ;
Her hopeless mind and heart were broken.
Still—still she mourns her beauteous seven,
And thinks they all were born in Heaven.

The Despondent Maiden.

"He had withdrawn Himself and was gone."—SONG OF SOLOMON.

(A very early Poem—Written in mid 'teens.)

• • •

ONE eve, where aromatic shrubs exhale
Their balmy odours to the gentle gale,
I saw a dreamy fairy maiden stand,
Her fingers toying with her silken band;
Dishevelled waves of nut-brown tresses shed
Their flowing beauty from her beauteous head;
So sweet—yet sad—in tissues white arrayed,
With beads coruscant round her neck displayed.
The moon's pale rays streamed o'er her features bright
As thus she spoke, in accents soft and light:—

   " Why, Queen of Warblers, why suspend
      The trillings of thy lay,
    Which many a time has been my friend
      And cheered my grief away?
    Oh, raise, sweet Songstress, raise again
    Thy ever fascinating strain

To soothe desertion's sting !
Alas ! the hour that e'er we met
He may but *I* can ne'er forget—
  Come, Queen of Warblers, sing !

" What—silent yet ? Then sweet shall be
  The wind's inconstant moan,
As changeful he who o'er the sea
  To other climes has flown.
With almond blossoms, whispering love,
The zephyrs play and fill the grove
  With music weird and wild ;
Yet what avail ? Since he is gone
I have no heart to lean upon
  Like his, so fond and mild.

" I long have loved to look upon
  Thy face, wan moon, so clear,
With *equal* smiles e'er looking on
  The gay, the wronged, the dear ;
But so inconstant, changing, cold,
As round in heaven thy orb is rolled—
  I scarce can love thee now ;
One while thou com'st all smiles and grace,
But soon thou hid'st in distant space
  Like him who won my vow.

" The flowers on earth again appear,
  But he comes back no more ;
The time of singing birds is here,
  But his returns are o'er :

Where'er he is, he draws me still
By beds of spice or gurgling rill,
  Or where sea-surges moan;
His banner o'er me seems to fly—
I feel his shadow, see his eye,
  And yet I'm here alone!

" While myriad stars look down on me
  And watch eternal keep,
I look in vision o'er the sea
  And watch—and wait—and weep;
' He hath withdrawn himself ' so far,
Like a receding, wandering star,
  Beyond the watcher's gaze;
His look on me with smiles—how sweet!
His voice—how pleasant—oh, to meet
  E'en after many days!

" Well, come, oh earth, be thou my bed—
  My lamp—the moon's soft beam;
One little hour I'll lay my head
  Beside this gentle stream:
Its rippling murmurs, calm and dull,
The yearnings of my heart may lull
  And wake fond dreams of *him;*
And when I wake, oh boon of Heaven,
If he to me again were given
  My bliss would reach the brim!"

Here ceased her griefs—her tears no longer flow,
She lays her down where flowers around her grow ;
The breeze in music through her tresses strays,
And o'er her form the chequered moonlight plays.
How beautiful on earth to see her sleep !
How sad on earth were it her *lot* to weep !
But—'tis not so ;—his ship has brought him home.
To where she dwells his steps immediate roam ;
Down in the gardens, past the lily-beds,
Straight through the vineyard, past the bowers he
    treads,
Near the bright rillet by the mossy bank,
Where, child of beauty, she so softly sank,
Bends o'er her form and marks her heaving breast ;
Fond, noiseless kisses on her brow are pressed.
Around her waist his loving arms are thrown,
She wakes, to feel, to see, to clasp her own !
No pen of poet e'er with graphic power
Could tell her raptures in that happy hour ;
Soon, soon was fixed the glad betrothal-tide,
And soon the bells rang welcomes to the bride.

Willie and Maggie.

HORACE, Book III., Ode 9.—*Free Translation.*

• • •

WILLIE—

While pleasant I seemed to you once, Maggie,
  For *me* while all others were spurned,
My heart was as gay as a king's, Maggie,
  With rapture it fluttered and burned.

MAGGIE—

As long as no lass but myself, Willie,
  Was pretty and sweet in your eyes,
My heart was as gay as a queen's, Willie,
  My joy into rapture would rise.

WILLIE—

A girl *far away* I love *now*, Maggie,
  Her beauty is thrilling to me ;
I would walk from the bounds of the world, Maggie,
  To seat such a girl on my knee.

MAGGIE—

A youth I have seen in the town, Willie,
  I love *him*—he's so grand and so fine;
I would walk from the bounds of the world, Willie,
  If only he would but be mine.

WILLIE—

But what if my love should *return*, Maggie,
  From her—the sweet girl far away,
Yes—what if her beautiful charms, Maggie,
  She *in vain* any more should display?

MAGGIE—

Though the youth I have seen in the town, Willie,
  Has looks, oh so winning, so sly!
With *you* I would live all my life, Willie,
  With *you*, not with *him*, would I die.

Lay of the Engine-Driver.

(PART SET TO MUSIC.)

* * *

I AM proud of my engine
  Brass-belted and bright,
For it lends me its speed,
  It lends me its might ;
With its long mane of steam
  In volumes unfurled,
Such a strong iron steed
  Is a boon to the world !

With thund'rous sound, that shakes the ground,
  Away, away we go !—
Snorting, glowing, rushing, blowing,
  Through darkness, storm or snow !—
On through gorges dim and deep,
Or where waters dash and leap ;
On through tunnels echoing loud,
Wrapt in flying steamy cloud—
  Away, away we go !

On through hills and by the shore,
Where the billowed waters roar;
On through rents of shattered rock,
Through the solid mountain block—
  Away, away we go!

As o'er landscapes I speed with a spirit of glee,
I revel with joy at the sights that I see!

  At the bounding of colts,
    Helter-skelter and wild;
  At the racing of lambs,
    And the play of a child;
  At the deer in a park,
    And the leaping of fawns;
  At the hounds in full cry,
    And the voice of the horns;
  At the hares on the moors,
    And the grouse in the heather;
  At the pheasants in stubble,
    With their young ones together;
  At the mansions of lords,
    Or a flower-mantled cot;
  At the doves in the woods,
    Or bright girls in a grot!

Such the sights I behold, just as scenes in a play,
And they vary, they vary each hour in each day.

Onward we rush
  To the neighing of steeds,
And the lowing of herds
  From their stalls or their meads.
The bridal group
  And the funeral throng,
Laughing or mourning
  We oft hurry along;
We bear the sick
  And we carry the dead
To sleep far away
  In the earth for their bed,
Where mortal sorrow
  Forever is o'er,
And Engine and Driver
  Are wanted no more.
At all seasons and hours,
  Through all weathers I go,
Be the nation asleep,
  Or the sun in full glow.
'Neath the stars when they shine
  All unnumbered on high,
Through the lightnings that fire
  The great vault of the sky;
Through the sleet and the fogs
  And the pitiless hail,
Through the peals of the thunder
  That roll down the gale,
I must still speed along,
  Just as if it were spring,

With its flowerets to bloom,
 And its cuckoos to sing !
I know I am rough,
 With my horny hands,
Like my Engine tough,
 With its brazen bands.

Yet should there hap the awful crash,
The screams, the groans, the fire, the smash,
My rough rude heart would thaw with tears,
And play the woman with grief for years.

But, guardian angels,
 Tend my train,
And let no life
 With me be slain—
With ceaseless watches,
 Hovering, wait,
And save from harm
 My precious freight !
My course through risks
 O'er all the line,
Oh, kindly guard
 With care divine !

'Twere well if at my journey's end,
To which all mortals' journeys tend,
I on my engine pause and pray,
And through the clouds to Heaven say :—

" Now done is my day's long task,
  Yet weary though I be,
One boon on my Engine I ask,
  Father above, of Thee !
As long as it is Thy will,
  I drive my daily train,
Go with me, oh Father still,
  And daily safety deign ! "

I am proud of my engine
  Brass-belted and bright,
For it lends me its speed,
  It lends me its might ;
With its long mane of steam
  In volumes unfurled,
Such a strong iron steed
  Is a boon to the world !

The Finger-Post.

• • •

HERE lone I stand, the wanderer's guide
  Through summer, winter, night and day;
'Mid gloom and glare, and frost and snow,
  To all who need I point the way.

Here comes a pilgrim bowed with years,
  And seeks of me which way to go,
And here, a group in want and tears
  Goes weary by—weak, worn and slow.

Sometimes a funeral-throng goes by
  With lingering pace, so dark and sad;
Sometimes a bridal hastens past,
  So merry, joyous, gay and glad.

Thus here I stand and thus survey
  The onward march of passing things,
The hurry, worry, pomp and sorrow,
  The moving scenes each morrow brings.

The Village.

* * *

Like a nestling bird the village lies
  Down in the valley, ever green ;
The gabled walls, the rustic thatch,
  Give homely quaintness to the scene.
The squire's hall at distance stands,
  The vicar's friendly home is nigh ;
No lawyers care to sojourn there,
  And Fashion ne'er goes flaunting by.

An ancient elm, the village pride,
  Towers high amid the village green ;
And round it oft the elders sit,
  And gravely talk of what has been :
While children to each other cling,
  As round and round the old elm-tree
They romp and shout, and dance and sing,
  In wildest, merriest revelry.

On Sunday, in the village church,
  You hear them sing—you hear them pray;
While all around them sleep the dead—
  The young, the old—long passed away.
They hear the preacher speak of Heaven,
  Where holy villagers are blest;
And hope, when all their lives are done,
  They, too, with them shall be at rest.

The Contrast.

(GRAVES OF THE RICH AND POOR.)

● ● ●

Beside a gorgeous sculptured stone,
   I saw a mother weeping;
Its golden letters simply told
   That there *her child* was sleeping.
Though high her rank, though grand her dress,
These did not make her grief the less.

Beneath a yew-tree's solemn shade
   Near by, I saw another:
There came a woman, meanly clad—
   She, too, a weeping mother.
A wooden slab—rough, rude, and bare—
Told passers-by *her* child was there.

There came some children richly robed,
   And joined their mother weeping;
They laid bright flowers of glorious hues,
   Where lay their lost one sleeping.
All wept their little sorrows there,
With mingled tears and flowers and prayer.

And children sought the *other* grave,
    Their scanty skirts in shreds;
They, too, brought flowers—forget-me-nots,
    And brilliant poppy-heads.
All these with tears they scattered round
Their little bit of sacred ground.

Thus, 'neath the purple and 'neath rags—
    Whatever garb we don—
Our common " kith and kin " prevails,
    And makes all hearts as one.
Our tears on grass or marble shed
Make *equal all* beside our dead.

The Watchers of the Deep.

(*FOUNDED ON FACT.*)

• • •

In darkest hours, while millions sleep,
  The lighthouse flashes bright;
There bide the " watchers of the deep "—
  Brave sentinels of night.
Far out at sea—aloft, alone—
  The tower on which they dwell,
By every raging blast is blown—
  Loud sounds its warning bell.

Full many a fearful night and day
  Two watchers watched up there;[1]
No food could reach them through the storm—
  No boats could succour bear.
At last the elder fell and died—
  The younger wept in dread;
By madness seized, he laughed, he cried—
  Left lonely with the dead.

---

[1] The Longships Lighthouse off the Land's End.

But when at length the storm passed by,
  Pale through the lantern streamed
The light of stars all round the sky,
  And o'er the dead man gleamed.
The Coastguard rowed in hope and awe
  To bring them off to shore;
But what a startling sight they saw !—
  What fearful freight they bore !
Let all, then, prayerful vigils keep
For storm-bound Watchers of the Deep.

Water or Wine.

• • •

AT feasts when I quaff, what, sir, should it be?
Oh Water, fair maiden, is fittest for thee!
   'Tis beautiful in springs and showers;
     How soft its fall as feathery snow!
   How grand its pomp of gorgeous clouds!
     What sparklings gem its brooklets' flow!
   There's beauty in its rainbow-arch,
     And in the dew the rosebud sips;
   With murmuring song its ripples march—
     Its crystal kiss best suits thy lips!

The choice then of Water of *course*, sir, is Thine?
Oh, no! my *own* choice,—it is *wine*—it is *Wine!*
   It sheds a golden haze on life
     And makes it all a happy dream,
   Adds lustre to a manly face,
     And makes the noble, nobler seem.
   It warms the heart with pleasant glow
     And gladdens man with jovial bliss,
   Makes eloquent the bashful tongue
     And cheers us with its ruby kiss!
Yes, the Wine-cup of banquets that kindles their glee—
Wine, wine is my choice—and no water for me!

The Fireman.

(SET TO MUSIC.)

• • •

HE comes, he comes, the Fireman brave,
Through burning chambers life to save!
His hatchet strong, his helmet bright,
His engine flashing far its light:
He comes, he comes—(God speed him well!)—
The roaring rage of fire to quell!

The ladder's dizzy height he scales,
Nor, girt with fire, one moment quails:
See—see him rush and bravely bear
Fair maidens down the burning stair!
Again he mounts—alas! to fall,
And perish 'neath the crashing wall!

HIS REQUIEM.

On the engine that brought him
From his home to his fate,
Marching slowly they bore him
To the grave's solemn gate:

Though no proud lettered marble
    May be raised o'er his head,
He will rank for his prowess
    With the braves of the dead.

Though resting now from Life's stern fight,
I seem to hear his engine's flight;
I fancy still I see him bear
A maiden down the burning stair.
He comes—he comes, dear lives to save!
Well done—well done, the Fireman brave!

The Nun and her Lover.

• • •

SADLY he calls back the time
  Elsie and he were yet young,
Played they and danced, and they sang,
  Sorrow behind them they flung.

Plighted they warmly their troth ;
  Oh, that her word she had kept !
Gave she another her heart,
  Faithless *he* proved, and she wept.

Cloistered in grim-looking walls,
  Penitent, now she's a nun—
Him she will smile on no more,
  Earth and its love she must shun.

Sings she—but never to *him*,
  Dance . . . she will never again ;
Cloistered away in those walls,
  Loving her now is in vain.

Yet there is joy . . . for the nun
  Leaves her old convent so grim,
Weds her first lover—still dear—
  Now, she is *happy* with *him !*

The Mechanics of England.

(Written many years ago, when the spread of knowledge among the Working Classes was thought to be dangerous.)

• • •

All hail, our Isle's Mechanics !
  The stay of Britain's power ;
Who make her strength still stronger,
  And stronger every hour ;
Whose engines ride all waters,
  And sweep the rolling earth ;
Whose glorious works have traversed
  All round this Orb's great girth.
Their skill has made more happy glow
Our English homes—the high, the low.

The clement that swings the stars,
  And that which sweeps each shore,
That awful thing that *warms* the whole
  And that the clouds hang o'er—

Yes, matter in its thousand forms
  Mechanics have to tame,
And bind and balance, curb and bend,
  And mould it to their aim.
Why, then, are all these "poohs" and "pshaws"
At teaching them great Nature's laws?

Come, England, then, befriend them—
  They are thy strong right hand;
They make the sceptre of thy power—
  By them thy power must stand.
Exalt their recreation
  (This greatly needs thy care),
With sounder education
  (This is their modest prayer);
They then with more enlightened skill
Can toil and serve their Nation's will.

Plaint of the Widowed Queen (Adelaide).

*(Written immediately after the Accession of
Queen Victoria.)*

Air—" The Light of other Days.'

• • •

THE eye of Albion's King hath faded—
  Its gentle light is past ;
And death in long, long night hath shaded,
  My joys too bright to last.
These pageants proud, thus darkly clouded,
  Late shone with brighter rays ;
But now I've lost, in sorrow shrouded,
  The light of other days.

How, radiant throne, thy glories wither,
  And pomp and power take wing !
Victoria, too, hath now come hither,
  All fresh in life's young Spring.
But now, while thus so deeply rueing,
  The wreck my life displays,
In my sad heart there's no renewing
  The light of other days.

Herod's Funeral.

* * *

VERY transient the glories that beamed
  O'er the phalanx that marched to his Grave;
Unsurpassed though the pageant that gleamed
  In the glittering ranks of the brave!

Steeled in mail, see his army appear,
  Proudly marshalled in battle array;
While his freedmen drop myrrh in the rear,
  And the Thracians his requiem play.

Richly chased is his bright bier of gold,
  Decked with tissue of Lydia's loom;
Richly wrought the fine purple, whose fold
  Now enwraps the dead king for his tomb.

Gayest blazonry spangles his robe,
  And his diadem circles his brow;
Now, how vain are that sceptre and globe!
  Not a slave will bow to him now!

Elegy.

(*On the death of a most devoted, popular, and beloved Clergyman, written immediately after his funeral.*)

" Qu'est-ce donc que l'instant où l'on cesse de vivre
L'instant où de ses fers une âme se delivre ?
Le corps, né de la poudre, à la poudre est rendu,
L'esprit retourne au ciel dont il est descendu."
—RACINE.

• • •

RAISED but to fall, he falls again to rise,
Though housed in death, his heritage the skies ;
His guerdon there, in loftier style to know
The great Redeemer whom he preached below.

The heart's lone dirge that, like a Spirit, roams
From cots and lowly hearths to prouder homes,
In voiceless grief, more deep than loud lament,
Bewails the tie the fatal stroke hath rent.

When hush'd the World 'neath Night's becalming
    sway,
To death-bed scenes he bent his solemn way ;
In dying chambers raised his cheering voice,
And pallid sick ones listened to rejoice.

Rejoice ! Alas ! for they will hear no more
The holy monitor they heard before ;
Lorn o'er the weepers broke his funeral knell,
And swept their spirits with its sadd'ning spell.

When in the depths of dark sepulchral shade,
With consecrating blessings he was laid,
His sorrowing people mourned a life too brief,
In dewy symbols of impassioned grief.

They to his church next Sabbath-day repair ;
The *Vacant Pulpit*—(what a loss was there !)—
Smote the grieved spirit with a sense to deem
Earth's greatness, ashes—human life, a dream.

The harp whence broke his simple gospel strain,
Save in heart-echoes, ne'er will sound again ;
Yet dear those echoes, though they bid one weep,
And through the heart in dying pathos sweep.

Yet wherefore mourn ? He bowed to God's behest,
Who yet will guard his sacred, lasting rest
Though o'er his dust the Grave's deep shadow frown,
'Till Time hath swept all generations down.

Yes, though it lie beneath the earth we tread,
Down in the silent chambers of the dead,
His soul will join the spirits gone that cry—
" Worthy the Lamb ! " and mount the echoing sky.

And when Creation's tottering bulwarks groan—
Worlds crash on worlds, and spheres o'er spheres are
    thrown—
God's potent Fiat, dread re-quickening power,
Shall wake his dust in Nature's closing hour!

Lauretta.

(*From the Italian—Free Translation.*)

* * *

To that high happy home where each spirit-elect
  Would go when it leaves us,
Thou, too, hast ascended, my own Gentle One,
  And thy going still grieves us ;
Yet down from the throngs of thy far Spirit-Home
To thy Earth-loved Lauretta I know thou wilt come.

Though with Cino, Sènuccio, and Dante thou dwellest,
  And the fair Fiametta,
All bright in the palace of Deity throned,
  Yet thou wilt not forget her ;
Though mingling with mysteries, joy ever springs
From thy deep-reaching ken of inscrutable things.

If this Earth's bosom-clingings are sweet in thy
 Heaven,
  If e'en there thou dost love me,
Still wandering below, with my thoughts ever driven
  To thy dwelling above me,
Oh, draw me in spirit, that once more I may see
The bright Being that first woke the fond passion in
 me !

Julia B.

(*A GREAT BEAUTY.*)

Lines supposed to be by her School-fellow.

(*Written by Request.*)

• • •

DEAR Reading's memories haunt me still—
  There we conned the lesson o'er;
Laughed or sighed with hearty will—
  Such days can come again no more!
From *me* thy lot has been to roam,
  The *school-girl*—now a *Bride* to be—
The Beautiful, in Beauty's home,
  Looking down upon the Sea!

All France hath not a gallant Son
  But would have woo'd thee if he dare;
How happy, then, the One who won
  The heart and hand of one so fair!
Heaven's blessings, Julia, now be thine,
  Though I again may see thee never;
May Heaven on Gerald richly shine,
  And both be happy now and ever!

Old Norwich.

(*A FRAGMENT.*)

*(Written, with the exception of one verse, between
fifty and sixty years ago.)*

● ● ●

QUAINT City of departed times,
  Full sad have been thy changes!
Dark-skirted oft by bannered hosts,
  Wild wrath in all their ranges.
With arrowy spire shot gleaming fire,
  And o'er thy walls ascended;
'Mid quivering flash and falling crash,
  The death-shriek weirdly blended!

Here came the Genius of the Plague,
  On gloomy pinion sweeping;
Where once were *crowds*—what silent *blanks!*
  In startled homes—what weeping!
Through murky night and day's silk light,
  What tears and sobs were gushing!
With fearful shock,[1] while Earth did rock,
  What crowds fled wildly rushing!

---

[1] While the Pestilence was raging, there was a fearful earth-
quake, and the inhabitants were naturally in a state of frenzied
consternation.

Whilst passing years have swept to dust
  Full many a generation,
Thou still hast mocked their mouldering might,
  Like the ever-fresh Creation !
In the wreck-strewn track of years long back,
  Though States have left no token,
We see that Thou art remaining now,
  With strong-built walls all broken.

But where are those long-vanished Ones,
  The first of all thy daughters,
That earliest strayed at eventide
  Beside thy Wensum waters?
In the quiet deep of church-yard sleep
  They long have been reposing ;
So on those who tread o'er the fair ones dead,
  The dust will soon be closing.

Oh, Norwich ! I must leave thee now,
  My sojourn well-nigh over ;
I gladly would re-visit thee
  When I'm no more a rover.
But the tide of change in Life's brief range
  May dash my hopes like bubbles ;
And the ties that once were sweetest joys
  Be numbered with Life's troubles.

The Ride to a Wedding.[1]

COMIC SONG.

(Set to Music.)

• • •

Now seventeen Ladies—each seventeen—
  A wedding went to see,
On fiery horses, sleek and proud—
  A maiden cavalrie.
Their hair all streaming on the wind,
  Like waves their habits flow;
Their joyous voices echo far—
  Their steeds most wildly go!

    Oh, stop, stop, stop, young Ladies!
      Don't trot, trot, trot, so fast;
      Or drop, drop, drop, you surely will,
      And roll on earth at last!

So, ho! there's one just toppled down;
  Two clowns to save her tried,
But, lifting her too high, too far,
  She falls on th' other side!

Written for and at the request of some College Students.

Q

But up she springs and mounts her horse
  And stops—oh no, not she !
The troop all helter-skelter speed,
  And chaff and laugh with glee !

    Oh, stop, stop, stop, fair Beauties !
      Don't trot, trot, trot so fast ;
    Oh, gal . . . al . . . al-op gently,
      Or down you'll roll at last !

Thus racing . . . at the Village Church,
  They halted in a jumble ;
But checking sharp their panting steeds,
  Ten had a comic tumble !
Then *in* they marched with whip in hand ;
  Confusion seized each Belle ;
The Priest and Choir were all amazed,
  The Bride—*she* swooned and fell !

    But up, up, up she rises,
      And trem-em-em-bled sore ;
    Then kiss, kiss, kiss-es follow fast
      When the marriage rite is o'er !

Then issue forth the maiden troop
  To mount their horses gay ;
But—ding, ding, dong !—those wedding bells
  Have scared them all away !

They bound, they fly, they rush, they shy,
  'Mid clouds of feathery foam;
No Legend tells how those fair girls
  That luckless day got home!

     Thus trot, trot, trot not, Ladies,
       So fast, a Bride to see;
     But wait . . . ait . . . ait at *home* till each
       Herself a Bride shall be.

Any Pans, Sir?

Words for Children to Sing or Recite at their Games.

● ● ●

Ladles and graters and pans, sir;
Shovels and trumpets and cans, sir.
    Will you buy—will you buy?

Candlesticks, colanders, pails, sir;
Whistles, as shrill as the gales, sir.
    Will you buy—will you buy?

Soldiers in tin, for the lassies,
In scarlet, or green as the grass is.
    Won't you buy—won't you buy?

Gems in bright tin, for your bride, sir;
Don't let your bride be denied, sir.
    Oh, for *her*—won't you buy?

Miss, pretty Miss, here's a kettle,
Nice when your wedding you settle.
　　　Oh, then buy—come and buy!

Pepper-box, canisters, knives, sir,
Sure to be liked by your wives, sir.
　　　Oh, then buy—come and buy!

Here's a tin hive for your bees, sir—
Charge you scarce nothing for fees, sir.
　　　Do, of your kindness, please buy, sir!

Here's a tin rattle, which *may* be
Far the best toy for the baby;
　　　Sure, it is *this* you must buy, sir!

Now, if my donkey should bray, sir,
This is just what he will say, sir—
　　　" Come and buy—come and buy!"

The Old Newspaper.

• • •

A JOURNAL old he finds
  Hid in an oaken chest,
A yellow, faded print
  With stains of Time imprest.
He sits and reads, and looks so sad,
  The old man in his chair;
Each crumpled page takes back his thoughts
  To times when he was gayer.

He reads of children playing,
  In that dim print of old;
Their memories all forgotten,
  Their history never told;
He sits and reads, and looks so sad,
  For he'd had children too;
With tears he lays the journal down
  Yet tries to read it through.

Some weddings there he sees;
  O'er all oblivion creeps;
He thinks of her he wedded,
  And when he thinks—he weeps.
He sits and reads, and looks so sad.
  For a burial-roll is shown,
It brings to mind all *he* has lost,
  For he is *left alone!*

An Old Man Stood in an Old Churchyard.

• • •

AN old man stood in an old churchyard,
　And leant o'er a grave-stone head;
'Mid all beneath him that slept around,
　He mused o'er the silent dead.
Bowed down, he prayed for the hour to come
　When he by their side should rest,
For weary now was his life to him,
　While *they* were so sweetly blest.

That evening sun was the last he saw,
　He died on that holy sod;
The star-light silvered his brow that night,
　Fetched home by the angel of God.
When dawned the light of the morning bright,
　His frail, withered form was found;
And the people knew that his prayer was heard,
　For rest in that quiet ground.

The Sculptor's Vision.

* * *

THE Sculptor felt her grace and power,
As sweet and fresh as loveliest flower;
    Soft on his heart her beauty dwelt
      As moonlight on a lake;
    But folded soon in arms of death,
      She slept no more to wake.
Long, long he mourned—unshared Life's cheers,
He wept for months—he wept for years.

Yet still her vision, ever bright,
Around him hovered, day and night,
    The marble 'neath his skilful hand
      Grew like her as of yore;
    It took her form, her face, her smile—
      'Twas She!—'twas She—once more!
Her image now he loved to find
For ever in that marble shrined.

Hibernia.

● ● ●

AH, me ! What maid in all the earth,
Since oldest nations had their birth,
   Was ever by such rivals flurried,
   Was ever by such lovers worried?
Yellow—Blue—their fond caressing,
Can I trust it bodes a blessing?

Though black as demons, some I know
Would have me think them white as snow,
   And promise me, in kindliest tone,
   A dear, sweet Parliament—my own ;
Though quite of late, in pure diversion,
They sought to coax me with "coercion."

But why this fussy stir for me?
Why bruit my name from sea to sea?
   Why, now the Yellow—now the Blue,
   Show each such care—such love anew?
Is it I'm made in Power's mad chase
A ready stepping-stone to Place?

That stepping-stone may arm with spite,
With wildest powers of dynamite;
    Let G.O.M. for place but fire the train,
    There'll be a blow-up—thousands slain;
Knife and pike, and blood in streams,
Dagger, bludgeon—groans and screams!

My own desire, my dearest Blue,
Is now to wed myself with you;
    I mean to jilt that "to-ther fellow,"
    That subtle soul, that wily Yellow;
His Home-Rule knife the tie sha'n't sever,
I'll cling to England now and ever.

Better with *her* make common cause,
And share the making of her laws—
    Partake *her* greatness, honours, power,
    Her statesmen shaking hands with ours,
And both combined to help each other,
As brother strives to help his brother.

With England better far unite,
Spite of G.O.M. and Parnellite;
    With her connected still to be
    In grand "Imperial unity,"
To share her Parliament and Queen,
And scorn the shams of College Green.

Love on a Lake.

• • •

FAR floating on a quiet Lake,
  As smooth as heaven's blue
(The Maid just past her girlhood bright,
  The Youth—as youthful too).
They sat, and whispering, side by side,
  Forgot to paddle on—
So great their bliss, the thought to row
  From both their minds had gone.

Their graceful forms the water's glass
  Reflected down below,—
Said He, "Your features on my heart,
  As *there*, in beauty glow."
"And yours, as in that Lake," She said,
  "Are imaged in my breast;
Dear—dearer far than all to me,—
  There, there, sweet Image, rest!"

Their troth was plighted in that hour;
  The quiet waters heard
The gentle utterings of their hearts,
  Their softest loving word.
And now the halcyon waters through,
  They ply the dripping oar,
To land on Earth—their Heaven now—
  Love's brightest, happiest shore.

• • •

THE Angel of Time that mars the scroll,
    On which men write
Life's fleeting glees and solemn doles,
    Its dark and light—
The burning seal of thousand suns
    On glory's dome
He sets, and then, like sands it runs
    To dust—its home.

The dome in dust—the scroll all marred
    Are both forgot,
With page and monument! 'Tis hard!
    What was—*is not!*
Well, *be* it so! Let columns fall,
    And marbles fade;
Let Time's dark mists o'erspread them all
    With death's deep shade.

Let chronicles archived in brass
    Unread—decay;
Their mem'ries, too, for me may pass
    From Earth away.
But written down in feelings deep,
    Mementoes done
By friends, those feelings still can keep
    Till Life's last sun.

Lo! one[1] which memory can't forego,
    Though, crumbling round,
Old Time his daily ruins throw
    Green on the ground;
Yes, Life may lapse, but yet, o'er all
    Its coming change,
This Gift will rise at Memory's call
    Through Life's long range.

So richly cradled, few have been
    Like Him[2] so blest.
He wots not *Who* has made the screen
    That shades his rest;
Yet after years—yes, after years,
    If they be ours,
Shall teach him *Who*—few be their tears
    On Life's young flowers!

---

[1] The Cradle.   [2] The Infant.

My happy pillowed boy—sleep on !—
    Thy cradle-bed
Will memoried be till I am gone
    Home to the Dead.
Dear Friends,[1]—oft hard the cradling found
    In human lot,
Yet soft be *yours* through all Life's round,
    Though I'm forgot.

---

[1] The Givers.

Then They must Go.

(Set to Music.)

• • •

Just as childhood's morn is opening,
    Bright with smiles and mother's glee,
Falls the shadow deeply darkening,
    Comes the stern "Thus far" decree,—
      Then they must go!

Bounds the boy in his young spring-tide,
    Skips the girl o'er Life's fresh dew,
Quickly ends the boy's glad bounding,
    Soon is blanched the girl's fresh hue,—
      Then they must go!

Just as maiden's love is dawning,
    Or as youth's first love is felt,
Droops the maiden like a flower,
    Wastes the youth like snows that melt,—
      Then they must go!

Oft as man his noon is nearing,
    Or as woman blooms in *prime*,
Sets *his sun* before 'tis evening,
    Fades *her bloom* before its time,—
      Then they must go!

PART VI.

• • •

Cities of the Past.

Ancient Athens.

" Peuples, rois, vous mourrez, et vous, villes, aussi ;
Là gît Lacédémone ; *Athènes* fut ici."
—RACINE.

*   *   *

THOUGH ages revolved but to heighten her glory,
  The sovereign of cities and boast of the Past,
Her pomps that are now but the record of story,
  Yet tell of the change that must conquer at last.

Where once Aristotle, deep musing, paraded,[1]
  No Peripatetic now lectures his train ;
Long, long has old Time the Lyceum invaded;
  Lone fragments of stone are all now that remain.

See how ye must vanish, ye monarchs of Reason,
  And all your proud marbles to ruin must fall ;
How men and their works have alike but their season,
  When Time o'er their wrecks spreads the dust of
    his pall.

The sweet wind no longer with blossoms is playing,
  Where once Epicurus set up his retreat ;[2]
Where olive-shades fell no disciple is straying,—
  The cool, classic groves echo not to his feet.

---

[1] Banks of Ilyssus.   [2] Gardens of Epicurus.

R 2

Bright garden of pleasure what change has gone
    o'er thee?
  Thy gay-blowing flowers now no more scent the
    breeze;
Thy beauty is withered—yet who would restore thee
  To shroud the famed sect in the shade of thy
    trees?

So in Eden no more shall we walk with our God
  In cool of the day, or the bright sunny hour;
Till waking from death, we arise from the sod
  To the Eden of angels, where death has no power.

How loud was the cry that triumphant ascended,
  When headlong to earth the quelled athlete was
    hurled!
But louder when Time, the great athlete, contended,
  The gymnasium crashed like the wreck of a world.

And thou dread Tribunal,[1] what sobs and repining,
  Where Archons once pondered the Fatal Decree!
A grave hast thou been, the old dead ones enshrining,
  Whose monuments shed their sad glory on thee.

From *His* Areopagus, last Judge of all,
  Jehovah, High Archon, each sentence will give;
To graves of long night all the wicked shall fall,
  No tombs will e'er rise where the righteous shall
    live.

---

[1] Areopagus, the supreme tribunal of Athens.

Twere sad to unfold the proud Parthcnon's changes,
  Queen-structure of Athens which nations might
      crave ;
Where Pagans now pray—now the Catholic ranges,
  'Till bow'd its great strength to the bomb of the
      brave.

Loud, loud over all, when her buttresses started
  The thunder of ruin re-echoed her knell !
Where now is her glory ?—forever departed—
  Though grand are the wrecks where the Parthenon
      fell !

On the banks of Ilyssus, soft stream of bright
      waters,
  That mirror'd great temples or sparklingly curl'd ;
Oft glided in beauty proud Athens' fair daughters,
  Whose graces have been the sweet theme of the
      world.

That " Fane to All Gods," the majestic Pantheon,
  With fabulous anuals all over engraved ;
Though pillar'd in power could last but its æon,
  Spite of gods and its columns it could not be
      saved.

The Temple, Creation, blue-roofed by yon arch,
  God's writing has covered—His great House of
      Prayer ;
All Worlds, its Processions, so grand in their march ;
  Its Lavas, all Oceans,—God's throne everywhere.

Here stood the *Death-gate*, where the dead were
    borne through,
Rich urns and tomb-altars encompassed it round;
The Gate has long fallen, and Time, as he flew,
    Down dashed all the tombs in sad wrecks to the
    ground!

But *there*, where the pearl-beams of glory are shed,
    Is the *Life-gate* of Heaven, with self-light all aglow;
Through *this* shall ne'er pass a dark train with the
    dead,
    Through *this* from our earth all the righteous
    shall go.

The Fane where the old Ocean-God was adored—
    Its salt-*spring* is dry, and its olive is dead;
From the *well* of the Church is the Spring ever
    poured;
    From the Olive set *there* is the life never fled.

Long lost is its Image that fell from the sky;
    Its Dragons are changed to the old Serpent's dust;
Its Lamp is gone out, its Oil-Vessel is dry,
    And the grave Symbol-Owl has relinquished its
    trust.

God's Image in man, though once lost, may be found;
    Sin's *Dragon* must plunge to the depth of his
    night;
The *Lamp* of the Spirit with oil shall abound,
    And burn in the soul with unquenchable light.

Thou Fane of the Mighty[1] —mortality's token,
  Colossal in fragments which mock at decay,
Thy columns half-buried, lie scattered and broken :
  Great Pageant of Power,—and art *Thou* pass'd
      away ?

Thus in crashings or calms, old religions have ended;
  Forts, palaces, temples, abide but their hour ;
The dust that is *past* and *to come* shall be blended,
  And be all that is left of the wonders of Power.

Old States, once so mighty, have left but a name,
  Dominions now great—all to nothing may fall :
Thus the greatest among us must go as he came,
  Till final forgetfulness cover us all.

O'er thy Poets, O Athens! thy Statesmen and Sages,
  Earth's mantle of dust was regretfully furl'd ;
Thy orators, first in the fame-roll of ages,
  Though mouldered to ashes, still dazzle the world!

Long gone are thy people, their altars and homes,
  Thy poor and their sorrows, thy rich and the
      great ;
Where once were their graves, now a modern race
      roams,
  And treads the old dust of thy relics of state.

---

[1] Great Temple of Jupiter Olympus.

Though ages revolved but to heighten the glory
  Of Athens "that *was*"—the proud boast of the
    past—
Her wrecks that are *now* the great wonder of story,
  Proclaim the sad fate that waits all at the last.

Jerusalem.

(A FRAGMENT.)

● ● ●

" Ecco apparir Gerusalem si vede,
Ecco additar Gerusalem si scorge,
Ecco da mille voci unitamente
Gerusalemme salutar si sente."
—TASSO's *Gierusalemme Liberata*.

OVER cities long fallen, with hoary caresses,
  The whitening weed twines and the ruin-worm
    creeps,
Or garlanded oft with its green ivy-tresses,
  A lone column is left 'mid the desolate heaps.

But down from her throne of the mountains des-
    cending,
  Oft toppling and ruined, Jerusalem fell;
Her ivy-wreathed towers, with Time long contending,
  Awoke in their fall the first sound of her knell.

Deep sunk in the gloaming of long vanished ages,
  Her first star of beauty no longer appears;
The pride of her bulwarks, her altar and sages
  Have passed on the echoless rushing of years.

Yet once, from her hills, like the morning light
  spreading,
 To the bounds of the world went the voice of her
  praise,
And chanting through deserts, lone pilgrims were
  treading
 To bow at the shrine of the "Ancient of Days."

'Mid the crumbling of ages undimmed was her glory,
 Generations saw holocausts smoke in her courts;
How grand was her Ritual . . . chequered her story!
 How desolate long lay her walls and her forts!

Though, peerless in pomp, bright and gorgeous in
  power,
 Her Temple was filled with miraculous gleams,
Though, curled round its columns the gold-fretted
  flower
 Crept sparkling beneath the Almighty's *own* beams.

No spirit-light *now* in that Temple is glowing;
 Its oracle silent as homes of the dead;
No altar the breath of sweet incense is throwing,
 The pride of its pageants forever is fled!

Yes, far o'er Jerusalem fearfully flashing,
 The Temple of God threw a fierce burning glare,
When, hurtling through Heaven, the dread sound of
  its crashing!
 Deep rolled its wild thunder-knell loud on the air!

But mosques of the Moslem, now crowning the
    mountain,
  Upheave where the grave of the Great Temple lies;
Beside them is playing the cool orange-fouutain;
  Not the *Cross* but the Crescent *now* gleams on the
    skies.

Now, shaded by citrons, the Mussulman kneeling,
  With the plash of ablution awakes a lone sound;
Whilst high from the min'rets in lengthened note
    stealing,
  The chant of Muezzins is floating arouud!

But who through the mists of bright mysteries to
    come
  Can see the Jerusalem yet that shall be,
When the Children of Zion, restored to their Home,
  Shall build their *New Temple* and *there* bow the
    knee?

Babylon.

(*A FRAGMENT.*)

* * *

" How is Babylon become an astonishment among the nations ! "
—Jer. li. 41.

Oh, thou that didst dwell on a throne of still waters, [1]
  That mirror'd thy Temples or sparklingly curl'd,
Proud palaces once were the homes of thy daughters
  And the light of thy glory beamed bright on the
    world !

Though the Giant of Glory, yon star of creation,
  Ne'er lit prouder towers through his all-circling
    sweep,
Thou art *now* but a wreck—a lone dank desolation,
  Where jackals are prowling and cold serpents creep.

In thy porphyry halls, with a golden light beaming,
  The harper woke sweetly the soft soothing strain,
But *now* they are fallen and night-birds are screaming
  Where the voice of sweet harpings will ne'er sound
    again !

---

[1] The Euphrates.

With desolate note the lone bittern is booming
  Where warbled so sweetly the bright birds of song;
Where the flowers of Chaldea once in beauty were
    blooming,
  The rank matted weed trails its dark length along.

Where the Voices of Nations once mingled in thunder,
  Wild beasts of the desert now startle the Night!
Thy walls, to all people a marvellous wonder,
  Have left scarce a wreck of their impotent might!

From the lair of thy ruins hyenas awaken,
  And aghast the lone Arab quails under thy brow;
Oh, Babylon—Babylon, why thus forsaken?
  The route of the caravan turns from thee now!

Great Queen of the earth, once the Empress of nations,
  The home of the mighty, the city of kings,
Down, down with the wrecks of all past generations,
  Thou art gone to decay 'mid unmemoried things!

But the knell of thy judgment forever is tolling,
  Thou Lady of kingdoms that quailed at thy nod,
Far, far to all ages its echoes are rolling:
  For thy greatness of guilt, overwhelmed by thy
    God!

PART VII.

•••

Libretti for Cantatas.

I.

𝕻𝔶𝔯𝔞𝔪𝔲𝔰 𝔞𝔫𝔡 𝕿𝔥𝔦𝔰𝔟𝔢.

DRAMATIS PERSONÆ.

PYRAMUS, *a Youth of Babylon.*
THISBE, *a beautiful Virgin of the same City.*
Their FATHERS.
Their MOTHERS.
WARDERS of the TOWERS.
The ASTROLOGER.
YOUTHS and MAIDENS—*Babylonians.*
MESSENGERS—CHORUS of HUNTSMEN.

THE Libretto for this Cantata is founded on the well-known Fable bearing the same name. The Fable was written about 2000 years ago and is recited in full in OVID, Met. 4., v. 55, &c.; HYGIN., Fab. 243.

It is one which appears to have struck the fancy of Shakespeare inasmuch as he has travestied it with inimitable drollery in his "Midsummer Night's Dream." In this work, however, in which it is used for the first time as the subject for a Cantata, the more tragic side of the story is taken. With a view to musical treatment several additional scenes and characters have been introduced, but yet such as the Mythologists themselves might presumably have employed had they drawn out the plot and scenes to their full issues. We thus obtain a more varied and elastic medium for the expression of passions and emotions than could have been the case if the treatment had been confined strictly to the narrow limits of the Fable itself.

8

ARGUMENT.

THIS, as represented in the Cantata, may be put as follows :—
Pyramus and Thisbe, both *illo tempore*, in the freshness and
beauty of youth, lived in Babylon, the ancient city of wonders,
through the midst of which flowed that historic stream, glorious in
its traditions, the river Euphrates.

Being natives of this place, they consequently dwelt in the
presence of the greatest triumphs of art and taste, and amid the
imposing grandeurs of the architecture of the period—in the
neighbourhood of

> " Gardens and pillar'd streets and porphyry domes
> And high-built temples, fit to be the homes
> Of mighty Gods."

They were most innocently and fervently enamoured of each other,
but their course of love was a painful and chequered one, and its
issue disastrous and melancholy.

Their parents forbad all interviews between them, and an astrologer further enhanced their pain and grief by affecting to discover
to their friends that the stars and fate were against their love
and union. In spite, however, of the parental interdict and the
oracle of the astrologer, and the warnings of the warders on the
towers against the danger of leaving the City-walls at night, they
appointed an interview in the dusk and obscurity of the hour of
danger at a sequestered spot some distance from the walls. The
place of rendezvous was to be under some mulberry trees that over-
shadowed the tomb of Ninus, the founder of the Assyrian monarchy,
and husband of Semiramis. At the intercession of friends of the
lovers, their parents agreed to withdraw their opposition and
consented to their betrothal. The knowledge of this consent was
purposely kept back from the young couple by their friends, who

simply wished to gain time for festive preparations and to make the announcement to them a greater surprise and joy. This kindly-intentioned purpose, however, was tragically frustrated, for, in the meantime, the unsuspecting and confiding lovers stole forth in secret at night never to come back again alive within the walls of Babylon.

Thisbe was first at the tomb, but, appalled by the sudden and unexpected approach of a great lion there, she rushes in terror from the place and seeks refuge in a safe hiding-place close by. In the confusion and terror of her flight, she lets fall her veil, an adornment so commonly worn by the Assyrian ladies in these remote times. The lion, seeing the veil, tears it in the fierceness of his fury and besmears it with blood, perhaps that of a recent victim with which his jaws were still wet. Pyramus next comes up and finding the well-known veil of Thisbe saturated with blood, concludes that the wild beasts of the desert had carried off her body and torn it to pieces. In his overwhelming desolation and despair, he feels he can no longer live in happiness or hope, and at once kills himself with his sword, falling dead on the spot. Immediately afterwards Thisbe, impelled by her fears and impassioned love for Pyramus, comes out of her hiding-place and again steals with soft and trembling steps to the shadows of the mulberry-trees by the tomb, but only to find the idol of her heart dead and weltering in his blood. Caressing his lifeless form and kissing his still warm lips, she takes his sword which lay by his side and plunged it into her breast, thus becoming his Bride and companion at least in death. The parents next approach the fatal scene and utter their mournful and inconsolable lamentations. In due course when arrangements were completed for the purpose, the Lion-Hunters scour the surrounding desert in search of the formidable beast that had brought such a woeful end to the love and life of the hapless pair, as well as to prevent a like risk and fate befalling others of the sons and daughters of Babylon. The bodies are borne to their last resting-place by affectionate and mourning friends, who sing a solemn Requiem in procession to the grave.

INDEX.

No.		PAGE
1.	INTRODUCTION (Instrumental)	277
2.	CHORUS (*or* Boat Glee)	277
3.	"IDOL-STAR OF HIS HEART" (*or* "Tho' temples high and bright")	278
4.	RECIT. AIR, "Song of Pyramus"	279
5.	RECIT. AIR, "Song of Thisbe"	280
6.	THE ASTROLOGER	281
7.	CHORUS, "Shall a crazy star-watcher"	282
8.	QUARTET, "Our son for Thisbe," &c.	283
9.	DUET, "Parted—parted must we be"	285
10.	CHORAL INVOCATION, "By the friends you love"	285
11.	THE MESSENGERS, "Raise your cheers"	286
12.	CHORUS OF JOY, "Ye youths and maids"	287
13.	WARDERS OF THE TOWERS, "Sons of the fearless"	288
14.	THE ALARMISTS, "I'll seek the halls"	288
15.	AIR—PYRAMUS, "Between the parting"	289
16.	RECIT., "With hopeful steps"	290
17.	RECIT. AND AIR, "With hushed and stealthy pace"	291
18.	AIR—PYRAMUS, "Death—oh, death!"	292
19.	RECIT. AND AIR—THISBE, "Again with timid"	293
20.	CHORUS OF LION-HUNTERS "Hunters, ho! away"	294
21.	QUARTET, "Death's blanch is on"	296
22.	RECIT.—THE ASTROLOGER, "Mockers of my sky-conn'd lore"	297
23.	CHORUS—PROCESSIONAL REQUIEM, "Slowly homeward we bear them"	298
24.	RECIT. AND AIR—THE FORSAKEN HOMES, "Deserted capitals—how soon they fall"	299
25.	CHORUS—FINALE, "Soft Nature weeps when love so true"	300

---

[1] Pyramus and Thisbe.

" IDOL-STAR OF HIS HEART."

*(Some Babylonian Youths or Maidens proclaim
the love of Pyramus for Thisbe.)*

Idol-star of his heart,
  Lily-queen of all flowers,
Dearest dream of his soul,
  Fairest belle of all bowers,—
Every smile was the sweetest
  E'er to youth had been given;
Round her Home was his Eden,
  And her love was his Heaven.

(Or this.)

Tho' *temples* high and bright,
And *palaces* of light,
  Fringed proud Euphrates' shore,
    So loyally, so loyally!
Her *cottage* 'mid the trees
He loved far more than these,
  Oft lingering near her door,
    So loyally, so loyally!

By vineyard, bower, or wells,
Of Babylon's bright girls
  That, tripping lightly, sing
    So cheerily, so cheerily:

The sweetest angel, she,
To thrill his heart with glee,
And on his love to cling
Unwearily, unwearily !

SONG OF PYRAMUS.

RECIT.

Tho' shadows cross my sky,
And hide each star above,
And cold winds nip the blooms—
Those flowers I dearly love ;
Yet wind nor shadow, frown nor cloud,
Can change the troth my Thisbe vow'd.

AIR.

Flowers !j ye sweet flowers, gay tho' your bloom,
Decking the altar and gemming the ground ;
Worn at the bridal and laid on the tomb,
Wreath'd, on the brows of the fair to be bound ;
Flowers ! ye sweet flowers—sweet tho' ye be,
Thisbe, *My* Flower, is the sweetest to me !

Stars ! ye bright stars, fair tho' your light,
Decking the heavens and gemming the sky ;
Wreath'd into coronals crowning the night,
Calm on the earth smiling down from on high ;
Stars ! ye pure stars—bright tho' ye be,
Thisbe, *My* Star, is the brightest to me !

SONG OF THISBE.

RECIT.

Though ruin swept the city,
  Its porphyry gauds and show,
Tho' vineyards cease to blossom,
  And fountains cease to flow;
His love will flourish still for me,
Though fount and vineyard cease to be.

AIR.

As doves on parapets of gold
  Soft coo their loving story,
Nor heed the birds of loveliest bowers,
  Tho' plumed in hues of glory;
So when he breathes the tale divine,
  More sweet than poets write,
I need none other, though he shine
  In gems of princely light!

A simple home with him to share,
  Were palace dear to me;
A palace proud, unshared by Him,
  Were home—*no* home to me:
Without Him dazzling pomps were dim,
  Life's sunlight ever gone;
But lowliest lot were bliss, with Him
  To lean my heart upon!

THE ASTROLOGER.

*(Interprets from the stars that the ruling of Fate
or Destiny is against the union of Pyramus
and Thisbe.)*

The subtle signs of dread portent,
From ghostly darkness upward sent.
Weirdest phantom, ... wizard's sprite,
Wail of cavern, ... spells that blight;
Dead men's glare, ... mystic sound,
Torch's flare, ... quaking ground;
Hence, hence my scorn! I use not these
To tell the fate of whom I please.
Where high in heaven the comet rolls,
I read men's dooms in starry scrolls;
Forecast the lot Eternal Fate
Assigns to each—his mortal state:
The fate of love . . . . 'tis mine to scan it,
In cycle, circle, star or planet.

Up there I read in letter'd light,
It is decreed in "Book of Night"—
They ne'er shall wed—a Fiat stern
No Gods can change, or Lover turn:
Their[1] fate in love . . . . 'tis *this!* I scan it,
In cycle, circle, star and planet.

---

[1] Pyramus and Thisbe.

CHORUS.

*(Of Friends of Pyramus and Thisbe inciting to
contempt of the superstitions of astrology.)*

Shall a crazy star-watcher
　Read up in the sky
What is wrapt in the future,
　Our fate to descry?
Shall the days of this youth
　Be thus ever saddened,
And his "Maiden of Beauty"
　Be nevermore gladden'd?
Shall their life's quiet morning
　Be marr'd thro' the spheres
By this crazy star-watcher
　In dotage of years?
Let them love and not care
　What stars may decree;
Let them love—let them laugh,
　All rapture and glee.

QUARTET.

FATHER AND MOTHER OF PYRAMUS
(*Contralto and Bass*).

FATHER AND MOTHER OF THISBE
(*Soprano and Tenor*).

Con. and Bass.   Our *Son* for Thisbe fondly burns,
Sop. ,, *Ten.*   - And *She* for *Him* in secret yearns.

Con. ,, *Bass.* -   *He* is our honour, pride and blessing,
Sop. ,, *Ten.* -   And *She* is worth a king's caressing.

Con. ,, *Bass.* -   But vain *Her* beauty without dower,
Sop. ,, *Ten.* - -   As vain *His* worth apart from power.

Con. ,, *Bass.* - -   We wish for *Him* a stately home,
Sop. ,, *Ten.* - -   And we for *Her* the pillar'd dome.

Con. ,, *Bass.* - -   We, jasper fountains must require,
Sop. ,, *Ten.* - -   We, porphyry chambers must desire.

Con. ,, *Bass.*   -   We—shining, tessellated floors,
Sop. ,, *Ten.* - -   And we—grand marble corridors.

Con. ,, *Bass.*   We wish for *Him* rich Arabesques,
Sop. ,, *Ten.*   -   And we for *Her* superb Moresques.

Con. and Bass. - - We—swiftest steeds of mettle bold,
Sop. „ *Ten.* - - We—blazing chariots flashing gold.

Con. „ *Bass.* *These* must be *His* ere bridal hour,
Sop. „ *Ten.* - - *These* must be *Hers* for bridal dower.

ENSEMBLE.

Con. and Bass. - - Our *Son* should wed your beauteous
Child,

Sop. „ *Ten.* - Our Child should wed your noble *Son,*

We know they love each other,

Con. „ *Bass.* - But, lacking riches, rank and state,

Sop. „ *Ten.* - - But, lacking riches, rank and state,

We seek for $\left\{ \begin{matrix} Him \\ Her \end{matrix} \right\}$ another.

PARTED, PARTED MUST WE BE?

*(Pyramus and Thisbe secretly appoint a place of
meeting.)*

Parted, parted must we be
  Like the fragments of a lute?
Broken all our hopes and vows,
  And our love forever mute?
No—for in the hush of night,
  We will meet by Ninus' Grave,
When the stars are shining bright,
  Where the mulberry shadows wave:
Softly we will pass the gate;
  Dull the watch the Porter keeps;
For we'll wander from the walls
  When the wearied city sleeps.

Mark—we meet by Ninus' Grave,
Where the mulberry shadows wave.

THE INVOCATION.

*(Addressed to the Parents by Youths and Maidens,
friends of the Lovers.)*

By the friends you love the best,
Some in sorrow—some at rest;
By your brightest bridal dreams,
And the hope that onward gleams;

By the spell of bygone things,
Still to which your memory clings—
Let your children join the tie
That shall link them till they die.

By the joys of happiest years,
Early sorrows—early tears ;
By the dearest things of time,
Those that cheer'd your morning-prime ;
By the sway of hopes to come
That shall rule your hearts and home—
Let them love, and let them woo,
As of old, *you* used to do.

THE MESSENGERS.

(*Several joyous Messengers in an ecstasy of gladness rush upon the scene proclaiming the good
news that the Invocation has prevailed.*)

Raise your cheers till Heaven is rent !
What you pray'd for, Heaven has sent !
Marriage bond and nuptial vow
Have their parents' sanction now.
Spread the spousal tidings bright !
Echo round the sweet delight !
Thisbe—happiest Bride of Earth,—
Hail her now with festal mirth !
Pyramus—her joy—her world,
Hail with cheers and flag unfurl'd !
Spread the spousal tidings bright !
Echo round the sweet delight !

CHORUS OF JOY.

(Occasioned by the good news of the Messengers.)

Ye youths and maids, with dance and song,
And voice of trumpets, trip along:
    Your garlands bring,
      Your banners fly,
    Let gladness gleam
      From every eye,
And merrily sing the song of glee!
Proclaim their spousals merrily!
As over domes . . . and over shrines
And gilded towers . . . the morning shines,
    Your standards wave,
      Your cymbals sound;
    Dance, dance and leap
      With joyful bound,
And merrily sing the song of glee!
Proclaim their spousals merrily!

Your palms and plaudits . . haste to bring;
Your wreaths and chaplets . . gaily swing;
    Swell, swell your cheers
      These happy hours,
    And strew their path
      With bridal flowers!
Oh, merrily sing the song of glee!
Proclaim their spousals merrily!

WARDERS OF THE TOWERS.

(Proclaim the perils of leaving the City at night.)

RECIT.

Sons of the fearless—lion-slayers,
 Go forth, and with resounding power,
 From us the Warders of the Tower—

PROCLAIM :

" Maidens of Babylon, beware !
 Grim jackals nightly stray and howl,
 And stalking lions surly growl :
 They haunt these walls and scan the Gate,
 Or deep in ambush couch and wait.
Maidens of Babylon, beware !
 And go not forth at twilight-time,
 But stay within till morning-prime."

THE ALARMISTS.

*(The Alarmists resolve to go to all parts of the
 City to notify the danger announced by the
 Warders.)*

RECIT. (*Tenor*).

I'll seek the hall where Beauties throng,
And weave the dance or trill the song—
 To raise the warning cry.

RECIT. (*Baritone*).

Where fountains gush in public Squares,
And fair ones flaunt on marble stairs—
   I'll raise the warning cry.

RECIT. (*Bass*).

To scarlet tents, where robes of snow
And golden tissues gleam, I go
   To raise the warning cry.

ENSEMBLE.

(*Tenor—Baritone—Bass.*)

In halls and cottage, tent and Square,
Ye Maids of Babylon, beware !—
Leave not these walls at twilight-time,
But stay within till morning-prime.

PYRAMUS.

(*Pyramus, impatient for the rendezvous with
Thisbe, is supposed to vent his feelings in the
following song.*)

   Between the parting and the meeting,
     How long the time we deem !
   Between the parting and the meeting,
     The moments ages seem !

   In dreams I feel her floating near me—
     A presence sweet and bright ;
   It lingers round my heart to cheer me—
     Dear Vision robed in light !

Speed on, ye hours—oh, speed our meeting,
 Where stars on mulberries gleam ;
Between our parting and our meeting,
 The moments ages seem !

RECIT.

*(Thisbe, not knowing her marriage with Pyramus
was now sanctioned, and not being apprised
of the warning not to leave the Gates at night,
goes out to meet him at the appointed place
and hour.)*

With hopeful steps and fairy grace,
She seeks at eve the trysting-place
    Where star-lit mulberries shone.

Soft, soft she says, "He'll meet me here—
My heart—oh, come!—the time is near—
    The moment hastens on!"
A lion stalks with stealthy stride ;
Appall'd, she feels him at her side,
    And like an arrow flees !
With bounding spring and fangs of gore,
Her fallen veil he fiercely tore,
    Then sped his prey to seize.

(Pyramus approaches, and RECIT. *continues.)*

RECIT. *and* SONG.

With hush'd and stealthy pace
He seeks the trysting-place,
His heart aglow and beating—
Soon, soon the joyous meeting !
Her love that hour did seem
His life's divinest dream ;
He waved the white-flower token
To words in music spoken—

" Come hither, come hither,
   Sweet joy of the grove ;
Come hither, come hither,
   Dear angel of love.
This—this is the *place*,
   The hour—it is now ;
Oh, hither—come hither,
   And plight me thy vow !"

But see—his glazing eyes !
All hope within him dies ;
For, lo ! the gory veil :
His swooning spirits fail.
Transfix'd and stunn'd as with a blow,
He stands—a monument of woe.

PYRAMUS.

*(At the scene of the supposed death of Thisbe—
believing she had been slain by wild beasts,
and that they had carried off her body.)*

AIR.

Death ! oh, death ! dread curse !
Wet with her life-blood
This[1]—this I see :
What—oh, what—has robb'd
Life of the chief good
That smil'd on me ?

Gone !—and no farewell ?
Lost !—and nothing left—
Only *this* token ?[1]
Her love !—oh, shatter'd spell !
How am I bereft,
And my heart broken !

Bright my days would flow,
Bright were she my Bride ;
Now that hope is past ;
Here from life I go—
Here where *She* hath died,
I breathe my last.[2]

---

[1] The veil.   [2] Kills himself with his sword.

THISBE.

RECIT. *and* AIR.

(Thisbe over the dead body of Pyramus.)

Recit.
Again, with timid fluttering heart,
She seeks the fatal spot ;
A piercing shriek ! a shuddering start !
Her risk . . . 'twas all forgot !
Prone o'er his lifeless form She fell,
And utter'd thus her heart's last knell—

Air.
" Think'st thou that She whose only light
In this dim world from thee hath shone,
Could bear the long, the cheerless night,
That must be Hers now thou art gone—
That I could live, no more to cheer
The last pure life that linger'd here ? "

Recit.
Her arms are folded round him now ;
She kiss'd his lips and stroked his brow ;
One prayer she breathes to yonder skies,
Weeps o'er his sword, then with it dies.

THE MOTHER OF THISBE.

(Over the dead body of her Daughter.)

AIR.

My beautiful ! my lost ! my beautiful !
Down on the green grass—dead ?
And no one near thee dying
To soothe thy spirit flying

Far to the ever fled !
  Why, slain by thine own hand,
  Thus seek the shadowy land ?
Dust to be now thy bed,
My beautiful ! my lost ! my beautiful !

Me all thy years have gladden'd,
  But, gone from this rude shore,
  Such joy is mine no more !
Now, will my years be sadden'd
  To see a life so bright
  Thus quench'd in sunless night.
What, to seek death, so madden'd
My beautiful ! my lost ! my beautiful !

LION-HUNTERS' CHORUS.

*(The fate of Pyramus and Thisbe, being attributed
  in Babylon to the sudden attack of a great
  lion, the Hunters go forth to track and kill
  him.)*

Hunters, ho ! away, away !
Sound the call to the mortal fray,
And speed along to the Hunters' Song :
          Away . . . away !
Soon the rush . . . . soon the clash,
Soon the awful mortal dash,
  The javelin and the spear !

Flying, glowing . . . . tearing, blowing!
  Thro' the marshes . . . thro' the bushes,
  Thro' the gorges . . . . thro' the rushes!
     Wildly bounding, on we go!
     Wildly bounding, on we go!

Coverts, caverns . . . . wildest, rankest,
Thickets, jungles . . . . densest, dankest!
  Burst them thro', burst them thro',
  To our thrilling, wild halloo!

Hurrah! hurrah! . . . . the game is found,
That awful roar . . . . it shakes the ground,
It rends the clouds . . . . that mighty sound,
It tears the skies . . . . it shakes the ground!

  With burning eyes, he death defies,
  And rushes, rages, springs—but vain,
  Tho' storming, streams his royal mane:
    The hunters' javelins, deeply thrust,
    Roll back the monarch in the dust!

QUARTET.

AN ELEGY.

PARENTS OF PYRAMUS (*Contralto and Bass*).
PARENTS OF THISBE (*Soprano and Tenor*).

Death's blanch is on $\left\{ \begin{array}{c} His \\ Her \end{array} \right\}$ brow ;
  Life's ties are wrench'd ;
$\left. \begin{array}{c} His \\ Her \end{array} \right\}$ silent lips are pale,
$\left. \begin{array}{c} His \\ Her \end{array} \right\}$ smiling glances fail,
  $\left. \begin{array}{c} His \\ Her \end{array} \right\}$ torch is quenched ;
Death's blanch is on $\left\{ \begin{array}{c} His \\ Her \end{array} \right\}$ brow.

$\left. \begin{array}{c} His \\ Her \end{array} \right\}$ pilgrimage is o'er ;
  Youth's bloom is cast ;
The loves of life are done ;
The things of death begun ;
  Time's bourne is past :
$\left. \begin{array}{c} His \\ Her \end{array} \right\}$ pilgrimage is o'er.

And now . . . . . the long farewell !
  Yet shall we spend
By Memory's well, sad hours,
And deck $\left\{ \begin{array}{c} His \\ Her \end{array} \right\}$ tomb with flowers,
  Till all shall end :
And now . . . . . the long farewell !

THE ASTROLOGER.

(Vain' of the accidental truth of his forecast that
Pyramus and Thisbe were never to be united,
complains of the slight put upon his warning.)

RECIT.

Mockers of my sky-conn'd lore,
Why my planet-craft ignore?
Skill'd in stars to read the fate,
Ruling mortal love or hate;
Riddles dark, occult and mystic,
Omens weird and cabalistic;
Oracles of constellations,
Planetary divinations;
Utterings dark of heaven's lips,
Sign or shadow of th' eclipse;
Or the comet's fiery flight
Thro' the complex spheres of night.

Why to wed them thought ye more?
Why my planet-craft ignore?

Fiat stern, the stars, I said,
Fated "they were ne'er to wed;"
Now their doom is with the dead.

PROCESSIONAL REQUIEM.

*(Youths and Maidens bear garlands and flowers
before the dead bodies of Pyramus and Thisbe
as they are carried in procession to the tomb.)*

Slowly homeward we bear them
　From Life's sunny bowers;
Slowly homeward we bear them
　With dirges and flowers.
What is mortal is over,
　Their "to-come" is begun.
They have launch'd on the voyage
　Afar from Life's land,
Where the Great Sea "Forever"
　Is bound by no strand.

We had twin'd for their *nuptials*
　These wreaths in their bloom,
Now we bear them in sorrow
　To garland their *tomb:*
With our torches inverted
　To be lighted no more,
We have now reach'd the Portal,
　Their Graves' solemn door!
In the earth here we lay them
　So fondly caress'd,
In the earth here we lay them,
　Here sweet be their rest.

THE FORSAKEN HOMES.

(Where Pyramus and Thisbe had lived, but whose associations caused their Parents to leave them.)

RECIT.

Deserted Capitals—how soon they fall,
And hoary lichens flake each broken wall!
So wild the aspect loveliest homes put on,
Whose sorrowing dwellers are forever gone!

AIR.

Sad the Homes from which they're gone,
　Where their love is ended;
Lone the walks they walk'd upon,
　Dead the flowers they tended.

Creepers dangle round the door,—·
　Where are they to weave them?
Laughter fills the Homes no more,
　Hard their lot to leave them!

Thro' the windows where they smiled,
　None see now their faces;
In the gardens growing wild,
　Blank are now their places!

Perish'd blooms the years restore
  Every Spring-time ever,
Here will they come back no more,—
  " *Gone from Home* " forever !

Sad the Homes from which they're gone,
  Where their love is ended ;
Lone the walks they walk'd upon,
  Dead the flowers they tended.

FINALE.

CHORUS.

Soft Nature weeps when love so true
Is blighted in its morning dew ;
When such pure lives as theirs are riven,
Which, joined as one, were sweet as Heaven.

Tho' some must *die* ere they be one,
And some must part ere life be gone,
With kindly lips as of a mother,
She bids them still love one another.

II.

David and Goliath.

• • •

CANTATA.

DRAMATIS PERSONÆ.

DAVID, *Shepherd Boy.*	JONATHAN, *Son of Saul.*
SAUL, *The King.*	WARRIORS.
GOLIATH, *The Giant.*	ABNER, *Captain.*
MICHAL, *Saul's Daughter.*	HERALDS.
COURT ATTENDANTS.	PRINCES and CAPTAINS of
MAIDS of ZION.	PHILISTINES.

(Between two mountains is the valley of Elah—
the Camp of Israel on one side—that of the
Philistines on the other.)

CHORUS OF ISRAELITES.

From yonder hill, far down the valley, leap
Goliath's taunts of scorn in thunder deep;
Our coward hosts feel *then* the mountains shake,
And at the challenge of his war-whoop quake;
In haste they flee before his horrent form,
Dread, vast and mighty, as a Fiend of Storm,

Saul (*to his Captains*).

Are ye the Captains of the Lord,
Yet tremble at this Giant's word?
Must *I* command 'mid slaughtered heaps,
As when I did down Bethel's steeps,
And drove the vanquish'd warriors through
All Gibeon's glades and Michmash too?
Oh, for a Hero-Captain bold
To lead my armies as of old!

(*Michal, Saul's youngest daughter and David's
future wife, approaches the Court and says*):—

My Father, cheer thee in this day of trouble,
  Think not thy glory flown;
Here's One with power and prowess double
  Will fight this foe alone.
No trumpet loud thy marshall'd hosts need call,
  These legion'd Philistines by *Him* must fall.

Chorus of Israelites.

No trumpet loud Saul's marshall'd hosts need call,
Yon legion'd Philistines by him must fall!
Though paths of war he never yet has trod,
Though but a child, he is the sword of God.
No clarion-voice—no trumpet-blast needs he
To win for Saul a glorious victory!

SAUL (*to Michal and the Court Attendants.*)

Alone !—a Samson, strong to kill—
Than strong Goliath stronger still ?
His aspect—is it savage, stern,
Goliath's boasts with scorn to spurn ?
Let me behold the dreadless one
That dares to fight the foe *alone.*

(*Michal and her friends, Attendants at the Court
of Saul, reply*):—

He is not stern, nor fierce in look or ways,
Nor savage in his deeds ;—
Aloof from city life he spends his days
In vales and flowery meads.
In shade of palms beside the brook,
He sings his Psalms and reads God's Book.
A ruddy youth and beautiful to sight,
Yet strangely arm'd with more than mortal
might.

(*David advances—Saul astonished at his simple
and youthful appearance.*)

SAUL.

My child ! . . . go home again !
Thy rosy bloom of face,
These locks of golden grace,
Ill suit the roar and rattle
And strife of mortal battle ;
They're not for warriors here,—
Play not with sword or spear,—
My child, go home again !

DAVID (*to Saul*).

My home is 'mid the pastures
     With my sheep ;
(I'm only a shepherd-boy)
     Them I keep,
And draw around me playing
     On my lyre,
With which the green hills echo.
     I desire
To make them my companions,
     Coming near
To rub their woolly fleeces
     'Gainst my knees,
And look me meekly in the face
     With loving stare.
We spend sweet hours together !
     Once a bear
One little lamb took bleating
     From the fold,
As also once a lion.
     Being bold
And strong with strength God gave me,
     I pursue ;
Though but a simple stripling,
     Both I slew !
In death I left them lying
     'Neath my blow,
And if thou wilt, I'll vanquish
     This thy foe.

(The Attendants of Saul to David and the Hosts
of Israel.)

Oh, fearless child
On whom hath smiled
  Thy Father—God divine;
Thy little hand
Shall rid the land
  Of this dread Philistine:
Then, if he dies,
Ye hosts arise
  And thankful victory sing,
Lift high the huzza
Loud echoing far
  To cheer great Saul, our King!

DAVID.

My flocks—I will leave them
  In their pasturage green,
Where God is their shepherd
  And there ever has been;
I know He will hold me
  In th' embrace of His power,
I know He will hold me
  In the perilous hour.
By Him safely shielded
  I will now go to fight
This Giant so dreaded,
  And so matchless in might.

U

(A group of Israelites—youths and maidens—
surveying the Camp of Saul at a distance.)

How goodly are the tents of Saul,
　On yonder mountain crest!
How brightly gleams God's holy light
　On every warrior's breast!
See there among pomegranate-shades,
　The chief in armour mail'd,
The Royal Camp—the flashing blades,
　The King with honour hail'd!
How beautiful the pomp of war,
　The march of thousands past,
The plume, the scarf, the charge, the shout,
　The thrill of trumpet-blast!

(A Warrior from the Camp, and Lady from
the Court.)

This youth leaves camp and king,
　The army's single van,
See—he approaches near
　Goliath—mighty man!
　　　His hair is rippling gold,
　　　His form is beauty's mould,
　　　His armour weak and slight
　　　To wage a mortal fight;
　　　And yet with prowess great
　　　He seems to court his fate!
A sling and stone are all he brings,
Child-champion of the King of kings.

(David goes fearlessly up to the Giant.)

DAVID—

> On yonder mountain many days
> I've heard thee jeering, call
> And mock the mighty hosts of God
> And his anointed Saul;
> Think not *I* quail, grim giant, gaunt,
> What is thy challenge—what thy vaunt

GOLIATH—

> Choose any man, your strongest, best
> To fight *alone* with me.

DAVID—

> Huge son of earth, vast Philistine,
> *I* come—*I* come to thee.
> *I'll* dare thy battle-challenge—
> *I ll* dare the fatal fray;
> Though shield and greaves I bring not
> Mere toys for giant's play.

GOLIATH—

> Thing of scorn, and *who* art thou
> Girlish ringlets on thy brow?
> Puny child from yonder host
> Lifting up thy baby boast;

u 2

Arm'd with little stick and stones—
Crash'd and smash'd shall be thy bones !
Daring *me*—a man of war ?
Vultures, flock and fill your craw !
Off !—begone !—or bird and beast
Shall make of thee their loathsome feast.

ENSEMBLE.

<table>
<tr><td align="center">*David.*</td><td align="center">*Goliath.*</td></tr>
<tr><td>

I come to thee with trust in God,
  He'll nerve my fragile arm ;
I fight for Israel's marshall'd lines,
  I fight, nor feel alarm.

</td><td>

I come to thee and trust *no* God
  But this my stalwart arm,
I fight for yonder Philistines,
  I fight and scorn alarm.

</td></tr>
<tr><td>

I come to guard the throne of Saul
  This Giant-foe to meet ;
My God's my shield, I cannot fall,
  He'll lay him at my feet.

</td><td>

To overthrow the throne of Saul
  This champion boy I meet,
With this my shield, I cannot fall,
  I'll lay him at my feet.

</td></tr>
</table>

RECIT., AIR, AND CHORUS.

RECIT.

Alas ! the sad unequal fray,
  As mightiest eagle with a lark ;
Alas ! so soon to quench his day,
  And hurl his spirit to the dark !

AIR—(*A sympathising Israelite*).

I love the golden morn of youth,
  Its sparkling spirits bright—
No shadow on its early dreams—
  No cloud upon its light.
I love the freshness of its life,
  The gladness of its spring,
The joyous beaming in its smiles,
  Its voice's happy ring ;
Why then to death send forth this youth,
  So bright and glad and free ?
Go, warriors go, and fight *yourselves*
  To gain the victory

CHORUS—(*Maids of Zion*).

Yes, go *yourselves*, ye warriors,
  And win your bays and palms ;
Your swords and helmets clashing,
  Shout, shout, "To arms, to arms !"
March, march, ye swarming legions,
  With blasts of trumpets shrill,
Blow, blow your echoing bugles
  To spread the martial thrill ;
Sweep *on*, like rolling rivers,
  Or *down*, like water-fall,
And crush the foe before you
  Till victory crown you all !
Go—go—and be your aim and joy
  To save from death this wondrous Boy.

(A Herald to the Hosts of the Philistines.)

RECIT.

Our Chiefs in Council held in state
Command our hosts no more to wait;
Goliath's challenge forty days
Has thunder'd where your weapons blaze,
And yet to meet our champion vast
A *child* is all they send at last:
At *once* then must the war-pipe blow,
The army on to victory go!

*(After the Herald's announcement to the Hosts,
the Princes and Captains and Leaders of the
Philistines urge them on to the battle.)*

CHORUS.

Warriors of our giant hosts,
  March to battle—march to war,
Israel mocks us . . . mocks our challenge,
  Every man his weapon draw!
Soldiers,—bright with serried shields,
  Legions . . . all with helmets crown'd,
Armèd files . . . with bristling spears,
  March with echoing thunder-sound!
Let your tread, ye brave battalions,
  Make the solid ground to shake,
Let your shout of thousand thousands
  Make the vaunting foe to quake!

On, ye mightiest troops of earth,
  Hurl defiance o'er the fields;
Let outfly your flaming swords
  Clashing on their sounding shields!
Blow the trumpets . . . blow the trumpets,
  Let the Heralds call "To arms!"
Lift the standards . . . lift the ensigns,
  March and gain the conquerors' palms!

DAVID'S PRAYER.

Mighty Father, be Thou nigh
While this mortal strife I try;
Wield my hand and nerve my heart
When this brooklet stone I dart.
He is strong and *I* am weak,
But my strength in Thee I seek;
He is great but *I* am small,
And without Thy aid must fall;
He has helmet, sword and shield,
I have but this sling to wield.
Mighty Father, guide my aim,
Down this champion bring to shame,
That the Philistines may see
There *is* no God to help but Thee.

CHORUS.

God be with thee, champion Boy,
  Our brother, hope and might;
God make thee stronger than our Hosts,
  And conqueror in the fight!

Great Arbiter of battle-strife,
Do Thou avert the blow,
That else must end his gentle life
And all his hopes below.

GOLIATH'S CURSE.

Dagon, Dagon,—hear me—
Fiercely with thy fiercest curses,
    Curse him ;
Fiercely in thy fiercest flames
    Immerse him !

Baal-zebub,—hear me—
Deadly with thy deadliest curses,
    Curse him ;
Down in Horror's darkest gulfs
    Immerse him !

Demons, devils,—hear me—
Ghastly with your ghastliest curses,
    Curse him ;
Down in whirling pools of fire
    Immerse him !

(*A sympathising Israelite.*)

SOLO.

The loves of Earth—
    Are they gone ?
The loves of Home—
    Has he none ?

No Father near
His lost child,
A straying lamb
Running wild?
His life is fresh
In its dew,
Why should his days
Be made few?
In his morning life
Who is there
Will keep him back
From the slayer?
The loves of Earth—
Are they gone?
The loves of Home—
Has he none?

THE BATTLE.

And now the issue draweth near,
The battle-test of sling and spear;
The Philistines the mountain crowd
And shout defiance fierce and loud;
The host of Israel list afraid,
Through all their trembling ranks dismay'd.
Now high his spear the giant shakes,
The failing heart of Israel quakes.
Goliath's armour gleams with light,
His brandish'd weapon flashes bright;
His coat-of-mail, his greaves of brass,
His fiery-burnish'd thick cuirass—

All blaze with brightness of the sun,
The battle-shouting is begun!
Yet David still remains unquail'd
Before the Giant-warrior mail'd.

The man of war with pond'rous tread
Stalks near to strike the stripling dead,
Uplifts his sword and wheels it round
To fell him headlong to the ground.

Now David takes his little bag,
At once his armoury and his flag;
A brooklet stone for little sling
He takes with little hand to fling;
With shake of waves of golden curls
The swift and fatal stone he hurls;
The Giant falls—his armies flee—
The Child has won the victory!

TENT OF SAUL.

*(Enter Abner, captain of Saul's Host; Jonathan,
Saul's son; and Michal, daughter of Saul,
David's future wife.)*

Trio.

Victory, Father, victory great!
Goliath just has met his fate!
Down he lies in yonder plain,
By the youthful David slain!

Fly the hosts—the Philistines,
Fast by Ask'lon's towers and vines;
But our soldiers hard pursue,
On their path the dead they strew.
Now our plaudits ring once more
As in victories won of yore!

(*Enter also David with the head of Goliath in
his hands.*)

My gracious King, I come not with a *Lamb*,
    As offering meet,
To lay in meek and loving homage down
    Before thy feet;
I bring this trophy, huge Goliath's head,
    So grim with death,
And which to carry here, so small my power,
    Took all my breath.
See here, these shaggy brows, what shades they
    cast
    As from a cloud,
This dark, dense shock of hair in which a storm
    Might seem to shroud:
This beard, so long, so broad, so deep, so black,
    Would scare my flocks
Through all their pastures, over knolls and plains
    Or down the rocks!
These eyes, when living, roll'd a startling fire,
    Now see how glazed!
The voice that thunder'd from these lion-lips
    Our hosts amazed!

This is the Trophy that, most gracious King,
          I bring to thee;
This great grim spoil of war—triumphant prize
          Of victory!

AFTER THE BATTLE.

*(Lamentation of Philistine Maidens on the death
    of Goliath and on the slaughtered soldiers,
    their friends and lovers.)*

The day is lost . . . a day to weep!
    Our army's heroes strew the plain;
Of stately forms and eyes of fire,
    Yet all their battling powers were vain;
The Conqueror God our thousands slew,
Oh, vanquish'd host,—we weep for you!

And shall we never see again
    Goliath great—our Prince of Might?
Nor those, the glory of our homes,
    The youths that were our love and light?
All through the dark pine-woods they lie,
Unburied 'neath the open sky.

Oh, Fathers, we your daughters mourn,
    Oh, Brothers, we your deaths deplore,
And Lovers, we your lovers yearn
    To kiss your lips once more—once more!
And now the long, the sad Good-bye.

(Saul to David.)

My gallant Boy, to thee we owe
Deliverance from this monster-foe;
This morning of thy youthful years
Has freed our quailing hosts from fears;
Thy prowess is a mystic gem
More glorious than my diadem.
Now give me, Boy, thy little hand,
That thus has saved our trembling land.
God crown thee with a bright reward;
For this thy deed I praise the Lord!

*(Call to render honour to the little
Shepherd-Conqueror.)*

Warriors, let the bugles sound
And the clarions echo round!
Let our marshall'd hosts acclaim
Wondrous David's honour'd name!
Let the maids of Zion shed
Blessings on his golden head!
We will strew his path with flowers,
Chant his deeds from royal towers.
Dweller in Saul's palace, He,
All his future years should be.
May his radiant fame resound
On to Time's remotest bound,

RECIT.

The Philistines like dew have thaw'd
And melted from before the Lord :
The host, acclaiming, high should raise
With choral joy its " Song of Praise."

SONG OF PRAISE.

Chorus.

" He hath triumphed ! "
　　　　Warriors sing,
　　　Praise our God,
　　　　The Heavenly King !
　　　Swell the chorus
　　　　Echoing loud,
　　　Let it reach
　　　　The hovering cloud !
Fear no foe whate'er his might,
If in God your cause is right.
Israel, lift the " Triumph song,"
For to God it doth belong !

" He hath triumphed ! "
　　　　Loud and long
　　　Blow the trumpets,
　　　　Let your song
　　　Swell in glory,
　　　　Roll along.
Wave on wave, till up on high
Your jubilations reach the sky !

" He hath triumphed !"
        Thunder . . . Thunder
        Like the sweep
Of sounding storm
        Across the Deep !
Let your voices
        Grandly roll
Loud and mighty,
        Fired with soul.
Praise in thousands—Praise the Lord
Who made the *sling* subdue the *sword.*

III.

Hypatia.

• • •

CANTATA.

DRAMATIS PERSONÆ.

HYPATIA, *a Pagan Beauty and Oracle.*
PHILAMMON, *a young and enthusiastic Monk.*
THEON, *Father of Hypatia.*
MIRIAM, *an aged Jewess.*
ABEN-EZRA, *a Jew, son of Miriam.*
AUFUGUS, *an old Abbot.*

CHORUS *of Alexandrians, Pagans, Jewish and Christian Mobs.*

PERIOD—5TH CENTURY.

THIS Libretto is a brief adaptation from some of the incidents of the Rev. Charles Kingsley's Work, entitled " Hypatia."

The dominant theme is the violent conflict between Pagans, Jews, and Christians, all striving for the mastery. Many characters in the original work have been necessarily omitted. Those selected have the same names in this Librettto as in Kingsley's book. A few original situations have been introduced as required for poetical treatment.

SCENE I.—BANKS OF THE NILE.

*(Philammon, in a papyrus boat, about to paddle
up the river to Alexandria—the aged abbot,
Aufugus, his life-long friend, sorrowfully
taking leave of him.)*

INTRODUCTORY CHORUS.

See the golden sun descending,
  Gilding Ægypt with his smile ;
See Philammon seeks the river—
  Seeks the waters of the Nile.
With him walks an ancient abbot,
  Sorrowful to say " Good-bye ! "
Down his silver beard is flowing,
  Down the tear drops from his eye.
Now Philammon nears the Ferry,
  Enters his papyrus boat,
Feels the Old Man's last caressings,
  Murmurs *this* " Good-bye " afloat :—

PHILAMMON.

My hermitage ! my hermitage !
  And thou, my dear and lonely cell,
Ye glens and tombs and haunts of prayer,
  I leave—I leave you all—Farewell !
        But Aufugus,
        Dear Aufugus,
        How hard on me
        To say to *Thee*—

x

Most loved—most holy anchorite,
My *first*—my long " Good-bye," good night !
It *may* be we no more may meet
In this, thy sacred blest retreat ;
   Then Aufugus,
   Dear Aufugus,
Most loved—most holy anchorite,
Once more—*once more*, " Good-bye," good night !

SCENE II.—THE GREAT LECTURE HALL IN ALEXANDRIA.

(Hypatia approaches to ascend the Tribune.)

CHORUS OF ALEXANDRIANS.

See she comes—a Grecian Grace !
Sweet the beauty of her face ;—
Ripples down with dazzling flow
Her Ionic robe of snow ;—
Golden hair in net of gold,
Figure tall—of matchless mould ;
Arms so beautiful and white,
Lit with glittering bracelets bright ;
Skill'd in deepest classic lore,
Skill'd the starry heights to soar ;
Sun or cycle, star or planet,
Wonderful her skill to scan it !
See she comes—her Lecture Hall,
Crowded as for festival ;
Monks and Jews and Pagans staid,
Throng to hear the Heathen Maid.

HYPATIA.

Above yon realms—above the night,
And all the higher spheres of light;
Behind the *veil* that Nature shrouds,
And mystic altars hid in clouds;
The dark mythology of things,
Its philosophic Gospel brings;
My dialectic proves it so,
From all the oracles I know;
The Gospel of the Gods of yore
Must claim your homage evermore.

PHILAMMON.

'Tis false—'tis false! In your own Hall
I come to cry: "Your Gods shall fall!"
Your priests their idols are forsaking,
Your altars in your temples shaking;
The Prince of Galilee is come
To overthrow all heathendom!

MIRIAM AND ABEN-EZRA (*Jews*).

This mystical maiden,
  Of all reasoners the queen,
This youthful Philammon
  With his famed Nazarene.
Shall they fight for their creed,
  Both the old [1] and the new, [2]
Crush out a creed older—
  The old creed of the *Jew?*

---

[1] Paganism.   [2] Christianity.

No! Heathen nor Christian, with fire nor with
　sword,
Shall ever supplant the elect of the Lord!

TRIO.

HYPATIA— *Heathen.*	MIRIAM— *Jewess.*	PHILAMMON— *Christian.*

Diverse tho' our creeds,
　Shall *that* keep apart
Our love for each other,
　All love from our heart?
Between the Immortals,
　And Moses and God,
Why brandish we thus
　The curse and the rod?

HYPATIA—　　⎧ Yet Heathens 　⎫
MIRIAM—　　⎨ Yet Jews, too, 　⎬ will riot.
PHILAMMON—⎩ Yet Christians ⎭

And ravage and fight,
And each will uphold
　His faith is the right.

HYPATIA—　　⎧ Yet Plato ⎫
MIRIAM—　　⎨ Yet Moses ⎬ divine,
PHILAMMON—⎩ Yet Jesus ⎭

Whose words are forever,
To slay for our creeds
　Forbids us *forever.*
Yet each the other's shrine would raze,
And guard his own with blood and blaze;

With riot, curses, axe, and knife,
Would force his creed with deadliest strife.

Hypatia— (Yet the Sage
Miriam— {Yet the Law } with the Olive
Philammon— (Yet the Christ.)

Might crown every brother,
And hand to hand link
Every one to another!

HYPATIA.

My childhood's dreams—my childhood's dreams
  All vanished, hopeless, dead!—
My ancient Gods, their cult and power
  Seem like a vision fled!
Sublimities of Pagan faith,
  Which erring mobs refuse,
Sublimer than the Christian's creed,
  Sublimer than the Jew's—
These—these by reason, myth and lore,
I fondly hoped I might restore.
But all my hopes are hopeless now!
  I quit my sinking throne,
For *all* religions *here* are wreck'd—
  Yes, mine—alas, my own!

Farewell old sages, priesthoods, thought,
Since mobs now reign where Gods have taught.

SCENE.

MIRIAM'S CHAMBER.—MIDNIGHT.

(*Miriam and Aben-Ezra.*)

Old Miriam, when the curse was done,
Saw peril to herself and son!
Their Race, with execrations knell'd,
The Patriarch Cyril had expell'd;
His *blood-hound Christians*,[1] beasts of prey,
Had sought to track them night and day:
In midnight hour and darkest gloom,
They[2] met in her most secret room,
And plotted thus to escape afar
E'er heaven reveal'd its morning star.

MIRIAM AND ABEN-EZRA.

Oh, let us to another clime,
  By stealthy bye-ways roam,
Where murdering villains will not seek
  A Jew's sequester'd home!
And, Guardian Heaven, hear our prayer,
  Protect us from the strife,
Of Monks and Pagans that alike
  Say: " Yield your creed or life!"

---

[1] Nothing could exceed the ignorant and remorseless ferocity of the Christians at this period.

[2] Miriam and Aben-Ezra.

THE MURDER OF HYPATIA.

*(Aben-Ezra and Philammon meeting under the
corridor of the Museum at Alexandria after
the murder of Hypatia, which both abhorred,
thus relate to each other what they saw.)*

ABEN-EZRA.

Frenzied the rush,
  Yelling the crowd,
Silver her chariot,—
  Murder was vow'd;
Madly her horse
  Lash-beaten, tore;
Down she was dragged,
  Saw I no more,
Save shreds of her robe
  All along thro' the street,
Poor relics for mobs
  To tramp with their feet!

PHILAMMON.

(Continues the narrative).

Onward they rush her
  Through the church-door;
In pressed her foes,
  Yelling yet more;

Up to the altar
  Blazing with light,
On yet they thrust her—
  Sad was the sight !
Incense and pictures,
  Lustres untold,
Pillars and shrines
  Fretted with gold !
Such sights were around,
  While, high above all,
Sublime was the Christ
  Looking down from the wall.
Upturning her face
  To the Immortals on high,
Yet stretching her hand
  Towards The Christ that was nigh,
Half-breath'd was her prayer,
  Yet, ere it was said,
A blow from a monk
  Prostrated her dead.

THEON, HER FATHER.

*(Struggling to the scene, he vehemently upbraids
her Murderers.)*

Oh ye Monks and ye Jews,
  Hateful demons of slaughter,
Bigot-slayers of *Truth*
  In its victim, my daughter !

Needs your Gospel or Faith
  Such a dark deed as this—
Down, down with them, Gods,
  To your lowest abyss!

(Turns and weeps over her body as it lies in
front of the Altar.)

My child, my gifted, glorious child,
  So pitilessly slain!
But speak, oh, speak once more to me,
  If only *once* again!
Oh let me kiss thy blanchèd lips,
  No more will they kiss me;
These lips whose words of living fire
  Will last all time to be.

In loving sorrow round my neck,
  Once more I lift thy arms,
In life so white, yet whiter now—
  Ah me, these clenchèd palms!
No more thy golden locks shall twine
  With these grey hairs of mine,
Whose flowing snow shall cover o'er
  Thy pallid face divine.
One kiss, my child, before we sever,
The last—one more—the last forever!
                       Y

CHORAL EPILOGUE.

As rocks hold firm to earth
  While ages slowly glide,
So races cling to creeds,
  Which firm as rocks abide.
The Pagan's faith hath sway'd
  O'er men and times untold,
The Moslem's too hath stood
  While centuries past have roll'd;
The Jew and Christian long
  Have battled with them all,
Before the Last, triumphant,
  All Gods and Creeds must fall.

Finis.

www.ingramcontent.com/pod-product-compliance
Lightning Source LLC
Chambersburg PA
CBHW031129120726
47905CB00006B/1615